Ginger opened the back door of the car and set the suitcase in.

"Thanks!" Mom said, then called back as they took off again. "I turned off the spaghetti sauce! Take good care of Lilabet!"

Ginger grabbed Lilabet's hand, and she didn't even object.

"They're gonna get that baby now," Lilabet said.

"Yeah," Ginger answered. "Yeah, they sure are."

Nothing would ever be the same again, she thought. Already that baby had changed things too much for everyone.

The Ginger Series
by Elaine L. Schulte

Here Comes Ginger!
Off to a New Start
A Job for an Angel
Absolutely Green
Go For It!

ABSOLUTELY GREEN

Elaine L. Schulte

A White Horse Book
Published by Chariot Books,™
an imprint of David C. Cook Publishing Co.
David C. Cook Publishing Co., Elgin, Illinois
David C. Cook Publishing Co., Weston, Ontario

Cover design by Ad/Plus, Ltd.
Cover illustration by Janice Skivington
First printing, 1990
Printed in the United States of America
94 93 92 91 5 4 3 2

Library of Congress Cataloging-in-Publication Data

Schulte, Elaine L.
Absolutely green / by Elaine L. Schulte.
p. c.m.—(A Ginger book) (A White horse book)
Summary: With God's help eleven-year-old Ginger balances her feelings of embarrassment and jealousy over her remarried mother's pregnancy and her feeling of dismay over her father's seemingly unsuitable new girlfriend.
ISBN 1-55513-758-X
[1. Christian life—Fiction. 2. Family life—Fiction.]
I. Title. II. Series: Schulte, Elaine L. Ginger book.
PZ7.S3867Ab 1990
[Fic]—dc20 89-33273
CIP
AC

to LB,
a special Ginger

1

Ginger Anne Trumbell sat on her bedroom window seat, chewing her gum faster and faster as she read. Vaguely she heard her mother's voice call, "Ginger . . . family conference in the living room! Everyone else is there already."

Ginger turned her book over and jumped up. "Coming!"

As she hurried down the hallway, she realized more fully what her mother had said—*family conference.*

Not once in the four months since Mom had married Grant Gabriel had there been a family conference, let alone in the living room. What could be so important?

Raffles, their old English sheepdog, rose to his feet in the entry, and Ginger gave his head a fast pat. "Good boy, Raffles," she said before hurrying on into the rather formal living room. Just this morning they'd taken down the Christmas tree, her big angel, and the olive wood creche. The room seemed sadly empty, even with her family waiting for her and a fire crackling in the fireplace.

"I was reading," she explained. "Sorry I'm late."

"No problem," Grant answered. He smiled pleasantly, looking more like a father than Ginger imagined most stepfathers did. "You know you can do all the reading you like in this house."

"It took a while for all of us to assemble," Mom added, her dimples deepening. She wore her blue Christmas jogging suit and sat close to Grant on the white couch as if they were still newlyweds.

Assemble for what? Ginger wondered as she flopped down onto the carpet. She glanced at the rest of them to see if they knew. Joshua, her twelve-year-old stepbrother, lay sprawled on the other side of the coffee table. He gave her a bored look. Lilabet, her three-year-old stepsister, jabbered with her mouse puppet, and Grandfather Gabriel sat back in the dark green wing-backed chair. He was probably ready for anything, since he was a retired minister.

Grant said, "I suppose you're all eager to know why we've called you together."

"We surely are," Grandfather Gabriel answered.

"We're waiting with bated breath."

No more changes; please, no more changes, Ginger thought. As it was, being eleven years old and part of a "blended family" hadn't always been easy so far.

Grant smiled again. "We thought we'd celebrate New Year's Eve with you right now, since Mom and I are going out tonight."

"You mean that's all it is?" Joshua asked.

Ginger felt a little disappointed herself. Why hadn't she noticed the cookies and bottles of sparkling apple juice on the coffee table? Maybe because they were partly hidden behind the basket of left-over red Christmas poinsettias.

"It's a bit more than that," Grant said. "We hope everyone will be as happy as we are with this news." He paused, then proudly added, "There's going to be an addition to the Gabriel family early this summer. We hereby and herewith and otherwise announce that we're going to have a baby."

"A *baby?!*" Ginger repeated.

Grant beamed. "Yes, a baby."

Ginger saw Mom's blue eyes turn to her, and then there was only the sound of the fire crackling in the fireplace.

Joshua guessed, "Are we gonna send money to adopt one of those orphans in Korea or somewhere?"

"Yeah," Ginger said. "I'll bet that's what it is."

"Not quite," Mom answered.

"No," Grant said, "we're actually going to have a baby."

"You mean, Mom's got a baby in her?" Ginger blurted. Heat rushed to her cheeks, and she felt stupid and embarrassed.

"The doctor says I most certainly do," Mom said, clearly delighted with her news.

You can't . . . you're too old, Ginger almost said, except that wasn't true. One of the girls at school had a mother even older than Mom who'd just had a baby. Still it didn't seem possible.

"What a way to start the new year!" Grandfather Gabriel exclaimed with his usual enthusiasm. "My second new grandchild in a year, counting Ginger! When is the baby due?"

Everyone talked at once, and Ginger heard something about mid-June and Grandfather say children were a blessing from God. All she could think was that life kept handing her one change after another: first there was Mom and Dad getting a divorce three years ago, then Mom and Grant falling in love and getting married last summer, and moving from the beach to live here with the Gabriels in Santa Rosita Hills—not that it was like leaving southern California, but it sure was different. As if all that weren't enough, now there'd be a baby, too.

Mom said, "I know this baby will bring us even closer together as a family. And you know how much we want that."

Ginger nodded, her feelings all tangled up.

Joshua said, "I hope it doesn't have Ginger's red hair!"

"Why, Joshua," Grant teased, "I've been hoping it would. You know how partial I am to red hair."

"Yeah, like Mom's . . . brownish-red and wavy," Ginger put in, serious. "I don't want any baby to look like me!" It was bad enough that she had wild, carrot-red curls, green eyes, and a straight-up-and-down body covered with freckles all over.

Grandfather said, "It's my guess that you were a very beautiful baby, Ginger."

Mom dimpled. "She surely was. Even strangers remarked about how cute she was."

Ginger felt a little better, though cute wasn't the same as beautiful. Still, she didn't think it'd be safe to wish for any shade of red hair for fear it might turn out to be as carroty as hers. "If it has to look like any of us," she decided, "I hope it looks like Lilabet . . . straight blonde hair and brown eyes."

Joshua asked, "What if it's a boy?"

"Then it could look just like you," Ginger said with a mischievous grin. "Straight brown hair and brown eyes . . . and wearing a diaper!"

Everyone laughed, and Grant said, "You asked for that, Josh! It never pays to tangle with a redhead."

"I'll get you later, Ginger Trumbell," Joshua muttered.

"Ha!" she returned. "Anyhow, if it has brown

hair, I think it should be thick and wavy like Grant's."

"That *would* be nice," Mom said with a fond look at Grant. "I wouldn't in the least mind a baby who looks like him. But I hope that it looks a little like each of us."

"Just so it doesn't have my gray hair," Grandfather joked.

Lilabet had been watching and listening without saying a word. Now she turned to Mom and asked, "You mean we're gonna get a doll baby?"

"No, Lilabet," Mom replied. "We'll have a real, honest-to-goodness baby. Ginger and Joshua have each other for company, and now you'll have a sister or brother closer to your age. A real baby like the ones we see at the church nursery."

Lilabet considered the matter for a moment. "I'm gonna play with that baby," she said with a firm nod of her head. "I'll say, 'Baby, let's go outside and play on the swing today. Let's go out and have a party with cookies and juice and . . . raisins . . . and black olives to stick on all our fingers.' "

Before anyone could laugh, Mom explained, "It'll be a tiny baby in the beginning. It will sleep a lot and only drink milk. It won't even walk or talk."

"Then let's get a *big* baby," Lilabet suggested.

Even Mom laughed at that. Usually she was very sensitive about people being laughed at, which Ginger appreciated because she hated to be laughed at herself.

Grandfather asked, "Are you feeling well, Sallie?"

"I feel wonderful, thanks," she answered. "Only a little thicker around the waist."

Grant said to his father, "Isn't she blossoming?"

"Yes," Grandfather said. "She looks just like an expectant mother should, all rosy and content."

Mom blushed a little and laughed.

That's why she's been looking prettier than ever lately, Ginger thought. Just last week at Christmas Grant had told Mom, "You look like a madonna."

Now he said, "We thought we'd keep the news until after Christmas. With the tree and decorations down, this gives us something new to think about."

"It certainly does," Grandfather said. He turned to Ginger. "Isn't this exciting news!"

"Yeah," she replied. She forced a stiff smile to her lips. "Yeah, it sure is." Only *exciting* wasn't the word for it. *Confusing* was more like it.

She glanced at Joshua. Her feelings might be confused, but his didn't seem too mixed up. Joshua looked plain upset.

"So is that all the news?" he asked.

"Yup," Grant answered with a chuckle, "that's it. We thought that'd be enough to hold us for a while." He began to open the slim green bottles of sparkling apple juice. "It seems a good time to drink a toast to the new year and to our new baby, since Mom and I won't be here tonight."

Ginger looked at Mom and Grant again. Mom

was handing around a plate of leftover Christmas cookies, and Grant was pouring the juice into the small glasses. Nothing seemed different about them except they were dressed in the new clothes they'd given each other for Christmas. Grant had worn jeans and a sweatshirt to take down the tree and the star from the roof, but since lunch he'd changed into the bluish-gray sweater and slacks Mom said matched his eyes. He'd given Mom the blue jogging suit to match hers.

Ginger had gotten used to their being in love, but now everything would be changing again. Worst of all, she worried that it wouldn't be as wonderful as they seemed to think.

"Here, Gin-ger," Lilabet said, carrying a glass of juice precariously. "Here's your juice and two cookies."

"Thanks," Ginger said.

"We're gonna have a real baby," Lilabet explained, her brown eyes bright with excitement.

"You're right about that, Lilabet," Ginger said.

Smiling from ear to ear, her little stepsister rushed back to the coffee table.

When they were all served, Grandfather Gabriel rose to his feet. "I'd like to propose a toast," he said in his nice, deep voice, "A toast to the new year ahead and to the new Gabriel baby . . . whoever he or she may be. And I ask for God's blessing on each and every one of us."

They all raised their glasses in agreement and, out

in the entry, Raffles woofed as if he understood.

Ginger sipped the sparkling apple juice. The bubbles tickled her nose as a thought hit. *Dad!* What would Dad think about Mom and Grant having a baby?

Something told her he wouldn't care for it very much. Maybe he didn't act like it, but sometimes he looked sorry about the divorce and that Mom had married someone else.

A new question hit. *Would he know about the baby tomorrow, when he took her and Gram out for New Year's Day dinner?*

And what about Gram . . . and the kids at school?

What would everyone say about Mom having a baby?

Ginger stared at the flames dancing in the fireplace. *Yuck on love,* she thought. *Yuck on love and babies and all of it. Yuck and double yuck again.*

2

They'd no more than finished drinking the New Year's toast than the phone rang. "Ginger, you're closest," her mother said. "Would you answer it, please?"

"Sure, Mom." Still in shock, Ginger hurried to the family room phone, Raffles at her heels. The phone was already on its fifth ring when she picked it up. "Gabriel residence. This is Ginger."

"Is that so, kiddo?" her father teased.

"That's so," she answered as if nothing were wrong.

"Don't forget dinner with Gram and me tomorrow," he said.

"I won't." *You're the one likely to forget,* she was

tempted to say, but resisted the impulse. Raffles had settled beside her, and she patted his head.

Dad said, "I'll pick you up at five o'clock. We're going to Filippi's for pizza, so you don't have to dress up."

"I'll wear jeans and the green sweater you gave me for Christmas," she decided.

"Hey, I'd like to see it. Bet it looks great with those green eyes and that wild red hair."

"I guess so." It sounded like he hadn't chosen the sweater, which wasn't surprising. Gram had bought his presents for him ever since the divorce and, before that, Mom had done it. Probably he'd never picked out a present for her, not even when she was little. Somehow she wished that he had.

"What's new, kiddo?" he asked.

Ginger blurted it out. "Mom's going to have a baby."

"A baby!" he repeated.

"Yeah, a baby."

The phone was silent until he asked in a strangled voice, "When's that?"

"In June. I—I guess I should have let Gram tell you."

He asked, "Does Gram know?"

"Maybe not yet." Even though Gram was her dad's mother, the divorce hadn't stopped her and Mom from being friends. "Mom and Grant just told the rest of us a few minutes ago."

"Well," Dad said thoughtfully. Then he added,

"I'll pick you up at five. I've got a big New Year's Eve date tonight."

"I'll bet." He had lots and lots of dates, but he didn't usually mention them to her.

He laughed, sort of a hollow laugh that made him sound like someone else. "Happy New Year, kiddo."

"Thanks. Happy New Year, Da—, I mean Steve." She still forgot that he didn't like being called Dad now because it made him sound too old.

The family conference in the living room was breaking up, and Mom carried the tray with glasses and the empty cookie dish into the kitchen. She was still beaming when she glanced at Ginger and asked, "Anything important?"

"Only Dad."

Mom's smile faded.

"He's picking me up at five for dinner tomorrow," Ginger explained. "We're going to Filippi's for pizza."

"Good." Mom's blue eyes met Ginger's. "Did you tell him about the baby?"

Ginger nodded. "Wasn't I supposed to?"

"It's all right. What did he say?"

"Not much. He just asked when."

"He had to find out sooner or later," Mom said. Before she was a Christian she'd probably have snapped, "Do you have to be such a big mouth?" or "It's none of his business!" but now she took what she called a longer view of things. She added, "Maybe I'll call Gram and tell her before he does."

Grant was just coming into the kitchen. He carried the empty sparkling apple juice bottles in his hands and Lilabet on his shoulders. "What's doing?" he asked, jouncing Lilabet up and down.

"Nothing much," Mom said, busying herself at the sink.

If it wasn't much, Ginger wondered, why did she feel so quivery and shaky all over? She said, "I've got to finish my book for a book report. It's due in two days."

In her room, she closed the door to the hallway behind her and locked the door to the bathroom she shared with Lilabet. Her best friend Katie always said, "Count your blessings," and Ginger was determined to try.

For one, the Gabriels were nice, even if they were a stepfamily. For another, she'd made friends at Santa Rosita Christian and liked going to school there. Another blessing was finally to feel at home in her peach and white bedroom. Sitting down on her twin bed, she suddenly saw it—especially the window seat wall and shelves—with new eyes.

It looked rather neat, even if her seashell collecton was dusty. The books stood upright, separated by pictures, driftwood, rocks, and her globe. Costumed dolls from around the world stood on the top shelf; another shelf held her stuffed animals: Spider, Octopus, Dinosaur, Fish, Fair Lion, and Parrot, who held the Bible verse card that began, "Put on the new self." Best of all, she liked the carved wooden angel Grandfather gave her for her birthday, and the wooden elephant she'd received from Katie's Great-aunt Alice, who'd died before Christmas.

As if those weren't blessings enough, there were trees and flowers outside the window, and a swimming pool beyond. Behind that was the guest house where Grandfather lived. *Ginger Anne Trumbell*, she scolded, *how dare you feel sorry for yourself just because Mom is going to have a baby!*

Going to the window seat, Ginger picked up *The Wind in the Willows*, which she'd been reading to Aunt Alice before she died. She settled against the pillows and decided to forget everything except the story; Mole, Water Rat, and Mr. Toad had problems, too. And Grandfather had said, "Hearing about others' problems helps to make our own more bearable."

As she opened the book, tears came to her eyes for no special reason. *Lord, please make my problems more bearable*, she prayed. *Help me to get through everything without feeling sorry for myself.*

"Happy New Year!" Mom and Grant called out the next morning at breakfast. They acted as though nothing had changed.

"Happy New Year!" Ginger replied, trying to sound happy.

After breakfast Grant spent the morning catching up on work he'd brought home from Santa Rosita Christian where he was the high school principal.

Grandfather Gabriel was writing a book out in the guest house. Joshua went to a friend's house to shoot baskets, and Mom sketched a picture of Lilabet out on the patio. As Ginger worked on her book report, she heard Lilabet ask Mom, "Where will the new baby sleep?"

"We're going to turn the guest room into a nursery," Mom replied. "We thought we'd use your old crib for the baby to sleep in, if that's all right with you, Lilabet."

Ginger could imagine Lilabet's turmoil. After a while Lilabet said, "She can sleep in my crib, but she *can't* have my yellow blankie!"

"That's generous of you, Lilabet," Mom said. "Of course, the baby can't have your yellow blanket. We'd like to use your old things for the baby, but not anything that's special to you. It's just like Ginger passing some of her things on to you when she's too old for them."

"Gin-ger gave me shells," Lilabet piped up.

"Exactly," Mom said.

When it was time to set the family room table for lunch, Lilabet told Ginger, "You gave me some things, and I'm giving the baby some things, but that baby can't have my yellow blankie or my Mickey Mouse hat from Disneyland!"

"Right, Lilabet," Ginger answered. "Especially not your Mickey Mouse hat."

The smell of toasted cheese sandwiches and hot tomato soup wafted from the kitchen, and Lilabet asked, “Can that baby eat cheese sandwiches?”

Mom laughed. She stood at the counter, flipping the sandwiches on the grill. “It’ll be a long, long time before this baby eats any sandwiches at all, Lilabet. Babies don’t even come with teeth!”

Having Lilabet around to ask questions made things easier, Ginger decided. Easier than having to think too much about the baby herself. She wondered if Dad would ask about it when he took her to Filippi’s for pizza tonight.

The front doorbell rang at five o’clock, and Ginger hurried past the entry mirror. She looked just right in her jeans and her new green pullover sweater; she’d even brushed her wild curls into what Mom called “temporary submission.”

“I’m leaving!” she called out to anyone who might be interested.

Ginger opened the door, expecting to see her father, but instead there was Gram. “Oh!”

“Do I look that bad?” Gram laughed.

“No,” Ginger answered, laughing herself. “You look nice.” Gram did look nice in a dark red pant-suit. Her white blouse had tiny red balloons held by brown bears—the brown to match her eyes. Her short salt-and-pepper curls shone under the entry light.

Gram said, “Your dad’s meeting us at Filippi’s, so I drove.”

“Oh,” Ginger said again. Gram didn’t like to

drive, especially at night, because her eyes were getting bad from her seamstress work. Besides, her car was a junker.

"Where's your mom?" Gram asked.

"Did I hear myself paged?" Mom asked as she hurried to the entry, followed by Lilabet. "I saw it was you from the kitchen window." She gave Gram a delighted hug.

Gram told her, "We just have a minute, but I had to see you for myself. You do look fine. In fact, you look wonderful!"

Mom nodded, all dimply. "I feel wonderful."

"Well," Gram said. "Well. . . ."

"That's a deep subject," Mom said with a laugh. "I don't think I've ever heard so many people say 'well' as lately."

Gram laughed herself. "And with one more 'well,' we'd better be off. See you at church Sunday."

In the car, Gram said, "I don't like it being dark so early this time of year." She made other remarks until she finally asked, "How do you feel about your mom having a baby?"

"Okay, I guess," Ginger said. It felt wrong to be so mixed up about it.

"It's normal to be a little jealous," Gram said.

"It is?" Ginger asked.

"It is," Gram answered. "It's perfectly normal." She kept her eyes on the road. "After a while, it'll be fun to have a baby. You'll see."

"I hope so," Ginger said. "I sure hope so." She hadn't realized that she felt jealous about the baby, but maybe she was. As it was, sometimes she felt jealous about having to share Mom with Joshua and Lilabet—and even with Grant.

When they arrived at Filippi's, the restaurant was already crowded. The smell of pizza, spaghetti, and lasagna made Ginger's mouth water. She glanced around and saw Dad standing up at a table near the back window, waving them over.

"There he is," Gram said, noticing him, too. "Did he tell you he was bringing a date?"

"A date?" Ginger repeated. "No."

"I expect he decided last night, because it wasn't in his plans yesterday morning," Gram said.

After he found out about Mom's baby? Ginger wondered.

She swallowed hard as she followed Gram between the crowded tables. Dad had *never* before brought a date with him when they went out.

Dad's smile flashed beneath his thick, dark moustache as he pulled out the chairs for them. "Hi, Mom," he said, then "Hi, kiddo. Hey, you look great in that sweater."

"Thanks," Ginger answered. He was more handsome than ever in jeans and a new tan pullover that looked perfect with his brown eyes and dark curly hair. He nodded toward his date. "Meet Danna Ulrich."

Ginger turned to the two-toned blonde who was

examining her. "Hi," Ginger said uneasily.

"Nice to meet you," Danna said with a small smile that didn't quite reach her eyes.

Ginger sat down hard, studying Danna, who was beautiful in an unusual way. Her hair, cut short in back, was glamorously full and carefully tousled on top; at the scalp it was almost black, then it became blonder and blonder, and you could tell it was planned. Her eyes seemed almost black at first, too, but they were actually a very dark blue. Her straight nose was perfect, and her rosebud lips were lined and painted a true red. She was lots younger than Dad, and Mom, too, for that matter.

"Danna works at the office at Santa Rosita Surfboards," Dad said. "She does some modeling, too."

"You look like a model," Ginger decided.

"Thanks." Danna smiled all the way to her dark eyes this time.

"I'm a seamstress myself," Gram explained. "I've always been interested in clothes and fabrics."

"Oh, really?" Danna asked, unimpressed.

"Well," Dad said as they lapsed into silence, and Ginger thought, *There's that word "well" again.*

After a while Ginger asked, "Where did you get that name, Danna?"

Danna raised her chin. "It's my professional name."

"Short for Dee Anna," Dad began to explain, but Danna shot him a stony glance.

Fortunately the waitress brought their menus,

and they all gazed at them as if they hadn't come for pizza.

When they'd decided on the Filippi Special, Gram asked Danna, "Where do you live?"

"Funny you should ask," Danna said, "because I moved into the apartment across from Steve's this week."

"Her family just moved to Los Angeles," Steve explained quickly.

"And I probably should have gone with them," Danna said.

"At least the traffic's not so bad here," Gram put in.

"Yeah, but there's lots more modeling and TV work there," Danna complained.

Gram said, "I expect that's so."

Dad told them, "Danna's taking acting lessons, too."

"What do you want to act in?" Ginger asked.

Danna raised her chin importantly again. "I'd like to get started in commercials and TV soaps."

"Commercials and TV soaps?" Ginger repeated.

Danna smiled and nodded.

Ginger almost said that no one at her house liked commercials or watched soaps, but she kept her mouth shut and spread her red napkin on her lap. She noticed that Gram didn't say anything either.

Ginger traced the red-and-white tablecloth squares with her finger. She began to think it'd be more fun to be home—even without pizza, her most favorite food in the whole world.

Finally the waitress returned, and Dad ordered the pizza and a large antipasta salad with four plates. After the waitress left, he asked Ginger, "You make any New Year's resolutions?"

"Nope. I've been so busy, I forgot." She considered telling him about Robin Lindberg from her class, who'd accepted the Lord at Christmas and had just moved back to New Orleans to live with an aunt, but Dad wouldn't care about that.

Gram said to Danna, "You're nice and thin—good for a model."

"I can't eat much," Danna said. "That's one of the hard things about it. I've got to lose five pounds now."

"You're already thin," Dad told her.

Danna said, "Yeah, but I don't want to get overweight."

Ginger thought of how soft and curvy Mom was becoming. Before long, she'd have a huge bulge in her middle. By comparison, Danna was b-o-n-y.

Dad said, "Danna and I sure did welcome in the new year last night."

Ginger didn't know what to say, so she stayed quiet again.

Dad and Danna discussed their date for a while, then ran out of things to say about it. Gram seemed at a loss for words herself, and Ginger stared at the green candle in a bottle in the middle of the table. Hot green wax rolled down and stuck to the old layers of wax, and somehow it reminded her of Dad, waxing over his problems with new ones . . . and this new one looked like it might be Danna.

Finally the waitress brought their order, and, as usual, Dad didn't say grace before they ate. Ginger prayed quietly, thanking the Lord for their food and asking Him to touch Dad's—and Danna's—heart, then bit into her first slice of pizza. Filippi's had the best pizza in town, cheesy and thick with sausage, pepperoni, and peppers, but it didn't taste as delicious as usual.

Looking at Dad over her steaming slice of pizza, she wanted to ask, "How can you like this Danna better than Mom?" Sure it was too late and dumb to think like that, but it didn't stop her from wanting to ask it and other stuff like "How come you had to get divorced and make everything change in our family?" Worst of all, she wanted to cry out, "Don't you even care that Mom's having a baby!"

3

The next morning when Ginger came to breakfast in the family room, Joshua looked sullen. Ginger doubted it had to do with returning to school, because he was smart and even liked to study. "What's up?" she asked, sitting down in her chair on the other side of Lilabet.

"Nothing," he mumbled and went on eating his cereal.

Lilabet, sitting high in her booster chair, said, "Josh-wa is bad. He says we're too old for having a baby."

"Yeah?" Ginger asked quietly since Mom was emptying the dishwasher in the kitchen. Luckily the dishes made a loud clatter.

"Yeah," Joshua answered. "That's what I told Dad. By the time I'm in high school, that baby is still going to be in diapers. And by the time that baby is in sixth grade, Dad's going to be fifty-two years old. If that baby goes to college, Dad's going to be almost sixty."

"I didn't think of that. Leave it to you, the math genius," Ginger said. "Did you tell them?"

"Yeah."

"What'd they say?"

Joshua shrugged. "Dad said they'd already considered all that, and everything was going to work out okay."

"So what's the trouble?"

"I said they were ruining everything for the rest of us!"

Ginger stared at him. Joshua might be grouchy sometimes but, according to Grant, he usually worked things out thoroughly in his mind. "What do you mean, ruining everything?"

"For starters, we won't be able to go on vacations or weekend trips or anywhere without dragging the baby along," Joshua explained. "Lilabet is just getting to be portable now. For a long time, she just lay around and yelled."

"Guess I hadn't thought about that," Ginger admitted as she helped herself to cereal.

Lilabet had been picking the raisins from her cereal. "I'm big now," she announced.

"Yeah," Joshua answered, rolling his eyes.

Ginger noticed that his brown hair, which he wore like Lilabet's in sort of a nicely done bowl cut with bangs, was beginning to get wavy. Except for his brown eyes and grouchiness, he looked a lot like Grant.

"What are you looking at?" Joshua asked.

"I was just thinking," she answered and began to eat fast. "For one thing, I wish we'd get cereals with sugar and honey on them. I get tired of nutrition."

"Yeah," he answered. "They worry about us getting hyper and ruining our teeth with sugar, but they don't care if we have to hear a baby yelling. Noise pollution."

Grant came in, dressed in his blue blazer and tan pants, looking like the Santa Rosita Christian High School principal should. "Good morning, all," he said, smiling as he sat down with them.

"Good morning," Ginger and Joshua echoed, but Lilabet asked, "Is that baby going to yell?"

Grant laughed. "I hope it yells just enough so we know what it wants," he answered.

Mom brought the coffeepot and joined them at the table, smiling joyously. "You yelled, too, Lilabet, when you were a baby. Each of us did, even Dad and I, when we were babies. But once children begin to talk, it's no longer necessary for them to yell. That's why we tell you to try to explain what hurts, even if it's your feelings."

"Sometimes Josh-wa hurts my feelings," Lilabet announced, crossing her arms.

Grant asked, "And do you forgive him?"

Lilabet shrugged and didn't answer.

Grant said, "It sounds like we need a special prayer this morning. Let's bow our heads."

Ginger stuck her spoon in her cereal. Usually each of them said grace quietly at breakfast, but she'd forgotten this morning, probably because of so much talk about the baby.

"Lord," Grant began, "we thank You for this beautiful sunshiny morning. We thank You for this new day, a special day to be used for showing Your love. We know we aren't worthy, Lord, but we are willing. Bless us this day and fill us with Your love for each other . . . and for everyone we meet . . . and for this new baby who's coming into our family. In Christ's strong name we pray. Amen."

When Ginger opened her eyes, she felt grateful for the first time in two days. It occurred to her that she hadn't thought to pray about the baby.

Even Joshua's attitude improved as they got into Grant's car in the garage. As they backed out into the driveway, Joshua asked, "Is this supposed to be a secret—about the baby?"

"Not especially," Grant replied. "Before long, everyone will notice Mom's middle expanding. Some of the other kids at school have new babies in their families, too. It's an exciting time, a special time for families."

Ginger hoped so. She sure did hope so.

They pulled up next door to pick up Ginger's best

friend, Katie Cameron. She'd just stepped out of the front door of her cream-colored, wood-shingled house, and she rushed to the car.

Grant said, "It's the first time Katie's been back to school since her Aunt Alice died. I hope everyone will be especially thoughtful."

"Yeah," Ginger said. Last week Katie had gone to Los Angeles with her family to help clean Aunt Alice's things out and make arrangements to sell the house and its furnishings.

"Hi, y'all," Katie said with her soft southern accent. She smiled at Ginger as she climbed into the backseat with her. Green was her favorite color, too, and she wore her green Christmas jacket, a matching plaid skirt, and green bows on her brown ponytails.

"Hi. I wore my new Christmas outfit, too," Ginger said. Gram had made the green skirt and matching flowered blouse, and the pullover sweater was the one Dad had given her.

"Welcome back," Grant said. "We missed you and your family last week."

"Thank you. I surely am glad to be back!" After buckling up, Katie added, "I do believe I'm gettin' used to this being home . . . even if people don't talk the way they do in Georgia!"

"I'm glad of that," Ginger said. "If you moved away, I don't know what I'd do." They'd only known each other since last summer when Mom and Grant were dating and Katie had moved in next door. Katie was her best friend ever, except maybe for Mandy Timmons, who'd moved to Chicago last year.

Katie looked pleased. "What's new?" she asked.

"Not much," Ginger decided to say. She glanced at the rearview mirror to see if Grant were listening, but he and Joshua were discussing the computer lab. Under her breath she said, "Have I got something to tell you later!"

Katie's brown eyes widened, but she didn't ask. After a moment she said, "The only bad thing about coming home is Aunt Alice not being there. I have to keep telling myself she's with the Lord now."

"Me, too," Ginger admitted. "Anyhow, I'm grateful I got to know her for a while."

They discussed undecorating for Christmas, then talked about Robin Lindberg moving back to New Orleans. Before they knew it, Grant had pulled into the parking lot in front of the white buildings of Santa Rosita Christian.

They gathered up their book bags and lunches, and started toward the buildings. At the place where they always parted, Ginger called to Grant and Joshua, "See you later!"

"Have a good day, girls," Grant said.

When they were out of earshot, Katie whispered, "What's the big news?"

"You won't believe it," Ginger began, "but Mom is going to have a baby."

Katie stopped. "You don't mean it!"

"Come on," Ginger urged, tugging her arm.

Katie moved forward with her. "Well, I'll be!"

"Yeah," Ginger agreed. "I was surprised, too."

By the time they reached the white elementary school blacktop, she'd told Katie all of the details. And by the time they headed for the flagpoles for the pledges of allegiance, she'd told Marcia Schiwitz and Cassie Davis, too.

Marcia, who wanted to be a nurse, said, "Wow, won't it be fun to take care of a baby!"

Cassie didn't seem as excited about it. "Sure, babies are cute," she said, "but it's a long time before you can really play with them. My little cousin is trouble, lots of trouble."

Marcia said, "But you can dress them all up and, if you're good at making faces, you can make them laugh like anything."

"What do you think about it, Ginger?" Katie asked.

Ginger shrugged. "I don't know. At first I was excited. Then Joshua said it'd always be bawling and a nuisance, and it'd ruin everything for the rest of us."

"Phooey on Joshua," Katie said. "My brothers didn't think I was such a good idea either, before I was born, but now they like me just fine. Maybe even a lot more than if I were their age. I'll bet Joshua will change his mind, too."

"I hope so." She'd hadn't even thought about Katie's brothers being older—one in high school and the other in college. "They do treat you like you're special," she said, "even if they tease a lot."

"What if my parents hadn't wanted to have me?" Katie asked. "Then where would I be?"

"Not here, I guess," Ginger answered.

Marcia asked, "What if our parents had all decided not to have us?"

"I never thought of that," Ginger admitted.

Mr. Adams, the elementary principal, called for attention, so they had to be quiet. He wouldn't be standing there either, if his parents hadn't accepted him, Ginger thought.

"Welcome back to Santa Rosita Christian," he said. "I hope you all had a wonderful Christmas and that you're eager to learn again. No announcements today, so let's begin with our pledges of allegiance."

Her mind still on the baby news, Ginger spoke automatically as they pledged allegiance to the American flag, but she still had to concentrate to remember the Christian pledge. "I pledge allegiance to the Christian flag and to the Savior for whose kingdom it stands. One Savior, crucified, risen, and coming again." It struck her that not one of them would be standing there if their parents hadn't wanted them as babies.

As they headed for their classrooms, Katie whispered to her, "You know what I was thinking?"

Ginger shook her head.

"God loves that baby already."

"You really think so?"

"Sure He does," Katie said. "Scripture says God

knows each of us as soon as we are knit in our mother's wombs."

"Then I guess He does," Ginger decided. She'd seen films of babies growing inside a mother's body. Probably by now he had little hands and feet, and his heart was beating like anything. She'd have to ask Mom how big he was and what he was doing.

In class, she headed for the back row and emptied her blue denim book bag into her desk. Then she sat down in her chair, between Jonathan Taylor and Daniel Wirt since Robin Lindberg was no longer there.

Miss Nordstrom stood at the front of the room. "Good morning to you," she said as the kids settled down. "Welcome back. I hope you all had a wonderful Christmas." She wore her bright blue suit and a matching ribbon to hold back her light brown hair.

She turned to Katie. "You have our sympathy, Katie. We all prayed for strength for you and your family, and that you could even be joyful about your Great-aunt Alice being with the Lord."

Katie sat in the second row, and Ginger saw her ponytails bob up and down. "Thank you," Katie said. "I knew you'd pray for us, and that helped a lot. We really were joyful, and at church the choir even sang the Hallelujah Chorus for her."

"Now that is joyful," Miss Nordstrom answered. She looked at the rest of them. "Anyone else have anything special to share?"

Kids waved their hands, taking turns to tell about what they did for Christmas.

At last Miss Nordstrom said, “Ginger?”

Ginger swallowed hard. “My mother . . . is going to have a baby.”

“How wonderful,” Miss Nordstrom said, “especially now after Christmas, when we've just celebrated the birth of our Savior. Are you excited about it, Ginger?”

Ginger thought about Joshua's sullen reaction and the way Dad had acted, then remembered how excited Lilabet was, and how pleased Mom and Grant and Grandfather Gabriel were. “Sometimes I'm not so sure how I feel about it because . . . it's still such a surprise,” she said. “But I sure do hope I'm going to like that baby.”

4

Ginger chewed her gum hard as she climbed out of Katie's mother's car with Joshua. "Thanks for the ride, Mrs. Cameron! See you, Katie!" She slammed the car door.

She and Joshua started down the shady lane of eucalyptus trees toward the Gabriel house. It was a welcoming sight for her now—a white Spanish house with purple bougainvillaea blooming against its walls, and red geraniums circling the green lawn. She suddenly felt like skipping, if it weren't for Joshua, who'd be sure to make fun of her. She glanced at him and found him frowning at her.

"What are you so grouchy about?" she asked.

His eyes flashed. "Did you have to tell everyone

that Mom's having a baby?"

"Why not? Grant told us this morning it wasn't a secret, and everyone would know by looking at Mom before long anyway."

"You don't know anything about what people might say," Joshua retorted. "You don't know anything, period."

"Mrs. Cameron thought it was wonderful when I told her. Anyhow, if you know so much about everything, why are you always spying on me?"

Joshua replied, "You spy on me and my friends, too!"

"I don't tease you in front of them, like you do me!" Ginger said.

"Well, you act so dumb sometimes that you need to know about it. And telling Mrs. Cameron about the baby was dumb."

"It was not!" She turned off his answer and was glad to see Raffles bowling along toward them like a shaggy gray-and-white blimp on legs.

"Woof!" he barked hoarsely.

"Hello, Raffles, old boy," she called out to him.

He stopped in front of them, panting and smiling through the shaggy hair that covered his face.

Ginger patted his head. "I know you'll like the baby, Raffles. I know you will."

"Ha," Joshua retorted. "Raffles will be jealous, just like he was when Lilabet was a baby."

"I'll bet you were jealous yourself," Ginger guessed. "I'll bet you were green, green, green with jealousy . . . absolutely green!"

"I was not!" Joshua objected. "I said Raffles was."

"Oh, yeah? How did you know?"

Joshua shot her a scornful glance. "You don't know anything about what it's like to have a baby. It's lots of trouble, I'm telling you."

"Mom's going to be here to take care of it," Ginger said. "If your mother hadn't died in that freeway accident, it wouldn't have been so bad for you when Lilabet was a baby!" The words were no more out than she saw Joshua's hateful look. "I—I'm sorry I said that."

"I'll bet!" Joshua snapped at her and rushed off.

"Come on, Raffles," Ginger said. "At least you love me, even if I am a big mouth."

Raffles wagged his tail-less rear end and woofed again. He panted beside her as they made their way through the pale January sunshine to the side of the house.

Ginger opened the black iron gate and eyed the familiar Gabriel sign. Grant said Gabriel was the name of an archangel, which was why his mother had collected angels before she died and partly why Ginger did now, too. If only she could be a little more angelic around Joshua!

Letting herself in through the family room door, she smelled meat and onions browning. Immediately, she began to feel better. One thing about Mom's cooking, you could smell and enjoy it a long time before dinner.

"Welcome home," Mom said from the kitchen, where she was chopping up carrots and potatoes on the big wooden block. "Did you have a good day?"

"Okay, I guess," Ginger answered.

Mom's blue eyes looked worried. "What's wrong with Joshua?"

"I guess he's just feeling grouchy," Ginger answered. She decided to change the subject quickly; one of the girls at school said her mother got sick a lot before she had their baby, so it was probably better not to worry Mom. "What's for dinner?"

"Beef stew, biscuits, and a tossed salad," Mom answered.

"Sounds good," Ginger said and reached for a banana from the fruit bowl on the counter.

Mom turned to the stove to stir the meat and onions. "I wanted to get an early start on dinner. I have to run down to the store when Lilabet gets up from her nap."

Just then Lilabet padded in, sleepy-eyed and barefooted. "Hi, Gin-ger," she said. "I colored in my coloring book today and we're going shopping and I'm gonna buy crayons and—and. . . ." Running out of words, she grinned at herself.

"You mean Mom's taking you just to buy crayons?"

"We need milk and lettuce, too," Mom explained. She poured water into the stew pot, making it hiss. "I'll put the vegetables in and turn it on low. Would you give it an occasional stir?"

"Sure," Ginger answered. "I'll do my homework on the counter here." Just so Joshua didn't start in again about what a nuisance a baby was.

Mom set the timer for ten minutes to remind Ginger to give the stew a stir, then she and Lilabet left for the supermarket.

Ginger spread her homework out at the kitchen counter and began to work on math. She was puzzling over a problem when the phone rang. She leaned over to answer it. "Gabriel residence," she said. "This is Ginger."

"That so, kiddo?" her father teased.

Trying to hide her surprise over his phoning so soon, she laughed. "Yup, that's so."

"I've got big news, kiddo," he said. "Big news."

Was he going to marry Danna? she wondered uneasily. No, he dated lots of girls and he hadn't married any of them yet. "What news?" she asked.

"Instead of traveling up and down the coast, I'll be working in the office at Santa Rosita Surfboards," he answered. "I'll be in town every Saturday, so you can spend them with me."

"You mean *every* Saturday?" Ginger asked.

"Every Saturday," he answered. "That's what the judge said I get. Your mother got custody of you, but I get visiting rights every Saturday."

Ginger felt her mouth dropping open.

Dad asked, "You still there?"

"Sure, I'm still here. I'm just surprised, I guess."

Suddenly the stove buzzer rang out raucously,

giving her an excuse to think. "Can you wait? I have to turn off the buzzer and stir the stew."

"No, I'm calling from work."

Ginger protested, "Have you talked to Mom about it?"

"Look," he said, ignoring her question, "Danna or I will pick you up at ten Saturday . . . every Saturday from now on. Dress casual, like jeans. See you then, kiddo."

The phone clicked in her ear, and the stove buzzer droned endlessly. After all of this time—over three years—he suddenly wanted his visiting rights. When she'd needed him, he'd always had more important things to do. But now that her life was beginning to settle down, he wanted to be in it—and to tear things up again.

Joshua burst into the kitchen. "Aren't you going to turn off the buzzer?" he asked.

"I—I forgot." Hanging up the phone, she hurried into the kitchen to turn off the buzzer. She twisted the knob and quiet filled the room. If only her heart could quiet like that, she thought. It hammered loudly as she removed the lid from the stew pot and began to stir.

"What's wrong?" Joshua asked.

Nothing much, she wanted to answer, but that was a lie. "Nothing I want to discuss."

"That's a change," he said, still looking mad. He grabbed an apple from the fruit bowl on the counter and headed back to his room.

The stew bubbled softly as she stirred, steaming her face and hair. What was it Dad had said? *Danna or I will pick you up?* Yeah. *Danna or I will pick you up.*

How could this happen on what was otherwise an almost ordinary afternoon? she thought. She wanted to see Dad . . . she truly did . . . but not with Danna!

Mom had invited Grandfather Gabriel for dinner, and he arrived at five-thirty, joining Ginger in the family room as she set the table. "Beef stew, one of my favorites," he said, inhaling the aroma with obvious pleasure. "How about you?"

"I like it all right," she said solemnly.

"Do I detect a lack of your usual enthusiasm about food?" he asked.

She shrugged, still upset by Dad's phone call. She hadn't mentioned it to Mom yet because Lilabet had been underfoot from the moment they came home from shopping.

His grayish-blue eyes probed hers. "Trouble?"

"Yeah."

"Do you want to talk about it?"

"I guess I'm going to have to." Mom was in Lilabet's room now, cleaning her up and taking a rest while she read to her.

Grandfather said, "Sharing our troubles with people who care usually helps. Do you want to see if I can help?"

"I don't know how to begin," she said. "And I don't want to worry Mom about it now that she's going to have a baby."

Grandfather Gabriel said, "You know I'll keep it to myself."

"I know." He was the first one to know she'd turned her life over to the Lord last August, and he hadn't told anyone. He'd said she should tell when she was ready, and that's what had happened. That short time of sharing with him on the beach had turned him into one of the best friends she'd ever known.

"Let's sit down on the couch," he suggested.

Ginger followed and sat down with him. "Dad called me this afternoon," she said.

"Your father?" Grandfather asked to be sure.

Ginger nodded. "He wants his visiting rights on Saturdays now . . . and I guess I have to stay with him and his girlfriend. Oh, Grandfather Gabriel, I do love him, but I don't want to be with him and that Danna."

Grandfather raised his gray brows thoughtfully. "I can't say I blame you for not wanting to go, but I'm sure your father loves you, too. Moreover, I do know he has visiting rights. I'm afraid you don't have much choice."

"That's what I figured," she said. "But what about telling Mom?"

"Let's just take one thing at a time," he suggested. "The first thing to do always is pray."

“Why didn’t I think of that right away!” Ginger said, discouraged.

Grandfather answered, “It’s not too late.” He held his hands out to her, and she took them.

“Lord,” he prayed, “You are the one who gives us peace, even in troubled times. Quiet our hearts now, we pray.”

Grandfather waited in silence for a long time, and Ginger’s heart did begin to quiet until she could hear only the soft bubbling of the stew in the kitchen.

“Thank You, Lord,” Grandfather said. “We know we are to thank You in all things, that we are to have an attitude of gratitude in spite of what happens. Sometimes we don’t feel like it, but we don’t know what’s ahead for us and You do. We pray that You’ll give Ginger thankfulness in her heart, even in this matter of having to spend Saturdays with her father and his girlfriend . . . something Ginger’s unhappy about, but must do. Use it to Your glory, Lord, and show her the best way to tell her mother. And, Lord, fill Ginger up to overflowing with Your joy, which we know comes from loving and trusting You. In Christ’s name we pray. Amen.”

As Ginger opened her eyes, she was shocked to see that Mom had quietly entered the family room. “Did you hear?”

Mom nodded. “I would have cleared my throat if you weren’t praying, but perhaps that’s no excuse. On the other hand, maybe overhearing the news in prayer was a perfect way for me to find out. I already know it's in God's hands."

"It might be that was how God meant you to hear it," Grandfather suggested.

"Maybe," Mom answered, then turned to Ginger. She opened her arms and caught Ginger up in them. "I love you," Mom said, holding her tightly. "I love you a million times more than you'll ever know. And, amazing as it seems, God loves you even more than that. He's going to help you through it. He's never let us down yet, and He's not going to. You know His promise—He'll never leave us nor forsake us."

Ginger's heart lifted, knowing it was true. Already God had taken care of part of the problem, letting Mom know through their prayer.

"An excellent sermon," Grandfather observed and added a hearty, "Amen."

Minutes later, Grant, Joshua, and Lilabet arrived in the family room for dinner. Grant looked at the rest of them, his grayish-blue eyes concerned. "Something wrong?" he asked Mom.

"Nothing that can't be solved by prayer," she answered. "I'll tell you later." She flashed him a confident smile, making him smile at her, too.

When they sat down for dinner, Grant said, "We haven't sung grace for a long time. Let's sing 'O for a Thousand Tongues.' "

They joined hands, Ginger between Grant and Grandfather, and sang out,

O for a thousand tongues to sing
My great redeemer's praise,
The glories of my God and King,
The triumphs of His grace.

Grandfather Gabriel smiled at Ginger, then at Mom. "How perfect that Grant would choose a song of praise.

Ginger knew it wasn't by accident, and the promise, *He'll never leave you nor forsake you*, echoed in her brain. A surge of joy flooded through her, and she hoped that Joshua might remember God's promise, too.

5

Despite Ginger's confidence on Tuesday, by Saturday morning she felt uneasy. For one thing, it was a dreary, rainy day. For another, Dad had said on the phone, "Danna or I will pick you up at ten Saturday."

At ten o'clock, she headed for the entry and peered through the small window in the Spanish front door. No sign of Dad . . . or of Danna. Ginger gave her gum a loud crack. She hoped Danna wouldn't come for her.

Five minutes later, she sat down on the entry floor in her yellow slicker. She opened her new *Victoria* novel and tried to read. After a while, she stood up and peered out the small window again. No sign of either of them. A good thing Mom was out running errands.

At ten-twenty, Joshua passed by and asked, "Where's your dad . . . out surfing in the rain?"

Ginger bristled. "He's just not here yet."

"Probably forgot," Joshua said nastily.

She'd already thought of that.

"Where'd he get that expensive red sports car anyway?"

It was none of Joshua's business about Gram lending Dad money so he could help start Santa Rosita Surfboards or about his getting big bonuses sometimes. She replied, "You sure are nosy, Joshua Gabriel."

Grant called from the kitchen, "Josh, why don't you help me fix this cabinet door in here?"

Joshua made a face at her as if it were her fault. Usually he had to help outside with yard work on Saturday mornings, but he couldn't mow the lawn in the rain.

At ten-thirty Dad finally drove up and honked. Relieved, Ginger put on her yellow rain hat and yelled toward the kitchen, "I'm going now! 'Bye!"

Grant answered, "Have a good time."

"Thanks." Probably he wasn't excited about her spending Saturdays with Dad, but at least he hadn't said anything to upset her. She stuffed her book in a pocket and, holding her slicker shut, ran out to the car through the rain.

Dad grinned as he leaned over to open the passenger's door. "Morning, kiddo," he said as she climbed in. "Don't get the car too wet."

"Hi," she said, slamming the car door shut. "I can't help it if I'm dripping!"

"Don't be so sensitive," he said. "I was teasing."

"Oh." She sat back and buckled up, thinking he looked wet himself. His kinky dark curls and thick moustache were damp, and so were his jeans and white jacket. He looked handsome anyhow, especially with a surfing tan in January.

"You the only one awake here?" he asked.

She saw him glance at the house through the rain before he backed up the car. "No, we've all been up for a long time. How come you want to know?"

"Just making conversation," he answered. "You don't have to get your back up about it, even if you are a redhead. By the way, you look like you're four years old in that rain hat."

"Thanks a lot." Ginger pulled off her rain hat and shook her curls loose. "Where's Danna?"

"Now who's asking questions?" he returned.

They sure hadn't gotten off to a good start, Ginger decided. She sat back in silence as they roared away.

After a while he said, "Let's try some safer questions then. For example, how's school?"

Not even that was safe, Ginger thought. He hadn't wanted her to go to a Christian school—not that he paid for it or anything else. She stole a sideways glance at him and saw he was just making conversation. "It's okay, I guess."

"Just okay?"

"Actually," she said, "I like it a lot."

"You're kidding."

"No, I'm not." The windshield wiper slapped back and forth, and she added, "It's the best school I've ever gone to, and I've made lots of friends."

"That so?"

"Yeah, that's so."

"We haven't really talked for a long time," he said.

"Nope, we haven't," Ginger agreed.

"I plan to make up for lost time now that I won't be on the road selling," he promised. "Guess what?"

"What?"

"We're going to spend every Saturday together until the end of time, that's what."

"Yeah?" she asked.

He grinned at her. "Yeah."

She sat back and glanced out at the rain. "I thought you said Danna might come for me."

"It was a maybe, but Saturdays are busy for her. She needs lots of sleep so she'll look good for modeling, then she's got her clothes and things to take care of."

"She too busy to see us today?" Ginger asked hopefully.

"Not that busy. Besides, I have to run in to the office for a meeting, and she promised to stay with you at the apartment."

"Oh," Ginger said, disappointed.

"We'll pick up hamburgers so she doesn't have to cook."

"Doesn't she know how?" Ginger asked.

"She doesn't have time to. We eat out a lot. Not like your mother, I guess."

"I guess not," Ginger answered.

Dad hesitated. "How's she feeling?"

"Fine as usual," Ginger said uneasily.

"When did you say the baby's due?"

She'd suspected he'd get around to that, though she didn't see how answering it could hurt. "The middle of June."

"Still over five months . . . a long time away," he said, his eyes busy watching freeway traffic through the rain.

If he asked one more question about Mom, Ginger decided she wouldn't answer. It was awful to feel like an in-between.

They stopped for hamburgers at McDonald's, then drove on quietly. After a while, he told her about his new apartment complex, Oceanview, which he called "exclusive." When they pulled off the freeway at the ocean exit, Ginger couldn't imagine what they'd talk about all day.

The rain still beat down steadily when they arrived at the Oceanview Apartments. Even from the car, she could see it was a beautiful place with a huge swimming pool and tennis courts. Dad said, "There's a game room with ping-pong tables, too.

We'll see if I can still beat the world's champion ping-pong player."

"I doubt it," she teased.

"Well, let's make a run for it, kiddo," he said. He tucked the bag of hamburgers under his jacket, and they climbed out of the car.

Ginger raced behind him through the rain and arrived at his patio out of breath. Under the roof, they took off their dripping rainwear. His outdoor furniture—white webbed chairs and a glass-topped table—looked expensive, too. Probably he'd gotten some nice bonuses lately.

"I don't have an ocean view," Dad said, "but I'd rather have a one-bedroom in an exclusive place than the penthouse in a dump, like where I lived before. That's why I never had you over. It wasn't good enough for you."

Ginger didn't quite believe it. "This is sure nice from the outside," she said. She felt strange, as if it were a place that didn't allow kids and the other tenants were staring at her from their windows.

He unlocked the door. "Wait till you see inside."

Inside, everything was white-white-white: entry tile, carpet, drapes, ultramodern couch and chairs, even the pictures.

"Now that *is* nice, isn't it?" Dad asked.

"I guess so," Ginger answered, worried about her slicker dripping all over the tile. "It looks expensive."

"It is," Dad agreed, "but I figure I deserve it after

putting up with that last place. All this needs now is designer plants."

"You can buy plants at the supermarket," Ginger suggested. "We got some yesterday on sale."

"No, that junk would spoil the effect." He began to take off his shoes. "We'd better take off our shoes since they're wet. We can leave them here on the tile. I'll hang our coats in the bathroom over the tub."

As she pulled off her slicker she asked, "When did you start to worry about getting things wet?"

He laughed. "Since I got nice stuff."

When he returned, he picked up the living room phone. "Let's see if Danna can come over." He eyed Ginger. "You need to comb your hair, kiddo. Bathroom's down the hall."

"If you say so."

The bathroom was all white, too, but with silvery streaks in the wallpaper and the matching shower curtain. Dad had hung her yellow slicker over the shower head, probably so it wouldn't spoil the effect. She found his hairbrush in the medicine cabinet and brushed her hair hard. She glared at herself in the mirror, feeling like her red hair and new green sweater and jeans spoiled the effect of the apartment, too.

When she found him in the kitchen, Dad said, "That looks better. Danna's hair isn't dry yet, so I figured just the two of us could eat lunch before I have to go to the office."

He'd set the white kitchen counter with shiny red plates and red glasses, and was reheating the hamburgers in the microwave while he poured their soft drinks. "You want to get chips and cookies out of the pantry?" He nodded at a nearby cabinet. "If not, I'll give you a knuckle rub."

She laughed. "Sure. No knuckle rub."

In the pantry, it wasn't hard to spot the Oreos and chips. The shelves were almost empty, except for pickles, olives, and a case of mineral water.

"Let's see if there's something on the TV," he said, flipping on the tiny countertop set. "Here . . . it's a kids' program. Now all we need is those hamburgers."

They sat down on the white and chrome bar stools, and Ginger bowed her head for an instant to say grace. She added, *And, Lord, please help me get through this day all right.* It wasn't much of a prayer, but Dad would be irritated to see her praying.

She'd seen the "Square One" show before, but she watched it again as they ate. The chips were fresh, lots better than the soggy hamburgers, and the Oreos were as good as usual.

When they finished, Dad looked at his watch. "I'd better get going to my meeting." He glanced at her. "I guess you'll be okay watching TV until Danna gets here, won't you?"

Her stomach was sinking, hamburgers and all. "I guess so. Anyhow, I brought a book to read."

"I'll write down her phone number, just in case."

"I'll do the dishes," she offered. There weren't many, just their two plates and glasses, and a few in the sink.

"Say, kiddo," he exclaimed, "you are growing up!"

Before long, he headed for the door. "See you soon," he said and dashed out into the rain.

She returned to the kitchen and began to do the dishes. After a while, she felt more at home and less abandoned. She was managing fine, even if it was a little boring. "Square One" was over, so she flicked the TV off, then went to get her book from her slicker pocket in the bathroom.

In the living room, she eyed the white furniture and decided to read on the floor by the front windows. At least Joshua wasn't around to tease her, and Lilabet wasn't yelling and driving her crazy. She settled down on the carpet and, after staring out at the rain on the patio for a moment, began to read.

It was a long time later that the doorbell rang. "Who is it?" she asked, getting to her feet.

"Hurry up, will you?" Danna called through the door. "It's still damp out here. My hair is getting ruined."

Ginger opened the door quickly. Her eyes went to Danna's two-tone black and blonde hair. "It still looks okay."

"Well, it might have stopped raining, but it's still damp," Danna complained. She plunked her plastic shopping bag on the entry tile and touched her hair lightly with her fingertips. "I'd like to murder your father for making me come out this afternoon."

"Sorry," Ginger apologized. She noticed Danna's perfect makeup, especially the red outlining her lips. "You really look . . . nice. Are you modeling today?"

Danna smiled and pushed back the sleeves of her black jogging suit. "No. But in this business, you never know when something's going to come up."

"Anyhow, I was all right here," Ginger said.

"That's what I told him."

Danna pulled off her black flats and lined them up on the entry tile next to Ginger's tennies. Even bending over, Danna was graceful, her every move perfect. "What have you been doing?" she asked, "Watching the tube?"

Ginger showed her the Victoria book. "Reading."

"Homework?" Danna asked.

"No, I just like to read."

"Yeah?" she asked suspiciously. "Well, I guess I can't blame you on Saturdays. There's nothing good on TV." Danna hesitated. "I hear your mom's having a baby."

"Yeah," Ginger answered.

Danna's dark eyes assessed her. "Too bad for you."

"What do you mean, 'too bad'?" Ginger asked.

Danna raised a sculpted, dark-blonde eyebrow. "I'm what they call 'a product of divorce' myself, and I know all about it. My mom remarried in no time, and the next thing I knew they had a rotten kid. Then the next thing that happened, my stepfather left because he couldn't stand kids!"

"My mom didn't remarry in 'no time,' " Ginger objected. "Besides, Grant's not like that."

"Oh?" Danna asked.

"Grant's—," Ginger searched for the words Grandfather used to describe someone like Grant. "He's solid . . . he has a sterling character."

"Ha," Danna answered, and it wasn't a laugh.

"Besides, I already have a stepsister and a stepbrother, and we're fine, just fine," Ginger said. She didn't want to remember how jealous she'd felt of Lilabet at first, or the trouble Joshua had been causing lately.

"So, think what you like," Danna said.

Ginger was tempted to fling an *I will!* at her, but she stopped herself in time.

Danna picked up her plastic bag and pulled out newspapers. "I brought some reading myself. You like the tabloids?"

"The tabloids?" Ginger stared at the newspapers she'd seen at supermarket checkout lines. "I've never read them."

Danna smiled. "Sometimes they're a little racy, but I'll let you read mine."

"Thanks," Ginger said, "but I'd rather finish my book."

"Well!" Danna returned. "If you don't mind!"

"I didn't mean anything wrong," Ginger put in quickly.

Danna's dark eyes studied her, then she said, "Guess I'll go in the kitchen and read. You can't read newspapers on a white couch anyway, and my black velvet outfit would pick up lint on the floor."

"I guess so," Ginger replied. Her mind churning, she tried to settle down on the carpet with her book again.

Danna called out from the kitchen, just around the corner, "You want any mineral water? Your dad keeps it for me . . . you know, for my diet."

"No, thank you," Ginger answered, then added a careful, "I'm not thirsty."

Danna turned on some light rock. "Hey, listen to what it says here in this tabloid. A man's head exploded when he sneezed!" She paused. "And here's another . . . a cow ate a farmer's wallet with nine thousand dollars in it. What I couldn't do with nine thousand dollars!"

Ginger thought, *I'll bet.*

Danna was quiet in the kitchen, probably reading. After a while she poked her head around the corner, carrying one of her papers. "You want to hear your horoscope?"

Ginger swallowed hard. "No, thanks."

"Why not?" Danna asked. "Do you have something against it?"

"It—It's against my faith."

Danna snapped, "How could your horoscope

have anything to do with religion?"

Ginger remembered what Grandfather Gabriel had said, and she told Danna kindly, "Astrology is occultish. God tells us in the Bible not to fool with it . . . or with witchcraft or . . . any of that. God loves us so much He warns us—"

"Really!" Danna interrupted, her nostrils flaring.

"That's what Grandfather Gabriel says," Ginger answered, suddenly nervous. "He's a retired minister."

Danna stared at her as if she might explode. "I'm not taking that from you! First, you think you're too good to read the tabloids, then you start on me over astrology and witchcraft! I won't stand for it, and I don't want to hear that Christian stuff!"

Danna slammed out of the apartment, and it felt like the door had slammed on Ginger's chest.

What had she done wrong?

She'd tried hard to say the right thing, but it felt terrible to have offended Danna . . . and awful to think what Dad might say if he found out!

6

"Didn't Danna stay with you?" Dad asked when he returned to the apartment.

Ginger was determined not to lie about the trouble, but she wasn't going to bring it up either. "She just left a few minutes ago." That much was true.

"Oh." Dad glanced at his watch. "We'd better get a move on, kiddo. Danna and I have an important party to go to in L.A. tonight. A good thing it stopped raining."

"I'll get my slicker," Ginger said with relief.

As she hurried off, another problem came to mind: What if they'd eaten dinner early at home? They probably thought she'd eat with Dad. It seemed like she caused trouble everywhere she went.

As they climbed into his sports car, Dad asked, "What do you think of Danna?"

Ginger slammed her door. "She's very . . . unusual."

Dad smiled. "I think so, too. She could go a long way in acting or modeling. She takes good care of herself, too."

"I guess she does," Ginger agreed.

As they roared out of the Oceanview complex, he added, "I'm sorry I had to spend all afternoon at the meeting, kiddo. But it'll be worth it in the end. We've finally caught the big wave at Santa Rosita Surfboards."

Rock music pounded from the car radio as he told her all about their new surfboards that had tested out well in Hawaii and Australia. Then he started in on the party they were going to tonight. Ginger sat back and relaxed a little; maybe he'd never find out about her trouble with Danna.

When they pulled up in front of her house, it was almost dark and the outdoor lights were on for her. "It sure was great to spend the day with you, kiddo," Dad said. "See you next week, same time, same station."

"Okay." It didn't sound like she had much choice. Climbing out of the car she said, "Thanks for the hamburgers . . . and for the day." She slammed the door shut and waved as the car roared away. At least she hadn't had to tell him about Danna.

Feeling like a stranger, she rang the doorbell.

"Ah, Ginger!" Grandfather Gabriel said as he opened it. "We were hoping you'd be home in time for dinner."

He was such a welcome sight that she felt like throwing her arms around him.

He grinned. "I'm here again for dinner myself. Your mother is afraid I'll starve if I'm left to my own devices." Closing the door, he asked, "How did it go?"

She smelled chili and corn bread, which made her feel better, and saw Raffles coming, wagging his rear end. It was such a relief to be home that she admitted, "Some of it was okay, and some was . . . not so good."

Grandfather asked, "Do you need to talk about it?"

"Maybe I do," she decided. She didn't really want to tell, but maybe she should.

Mom and Grant arrived in the entry. "You're just in time to eat," Mom said with a smile.

Ginger tried to smile, but her lips were stiff.

Mom turned serious. "Uh-oh . . . trouble?"

Ginger shrugged. "I don't know."

"Have you discussed it with your father?" Mom asked.

Ginger shook her head. "I didn't want him to know."

"Oh, Ginger!" Mom said and gave her a hug. She stood back, her eyes full of concern. "We don't want to pry . . . I hope you can understand that. Divorce causes so many difficult situations, and I wish. . . ." She paused and let out a deep breath. "Well, we can't change the past, but I do wish it didn't have to complicate your life now."

"Do you want to talk to your mother alone?" Grant asked.

"I think I need to tell all of you, but—" Her voice trembled a little, "I—I don't want Joshua to know."

"Let's go into the living room then," Mom suggested.

"Josh is in his room doing homework," Grant said, "and Lilabet is watching *Mary Poppins* again."

Grant and Mom turned on the living room lights. As Ginger sat down between them on the couch, it occurred to her that just a week ago they'd met in this room for the family conference about having the baby. After that came the trouble with Dad, and now this problem with Danna.

Grant said, "It's a difficult situation for you and for us, Ginger, but our main interest is your welfare. I hope you know how deeply we care about you."

She nodded, not knowing where to begin. She decided to start with having hamburgers for lunch before Dad left, then Danna's arrival. Ginger grabbed a deep breath. "Everything was fine at first, but then Danna started telling me your having a baby would ruin everything, and I told her it wouldn't be like that in this family. I didn't argue or anything. After a while, she wanted to read me my horoscope, and that's when the real trouble began."

She told everything she could remember and finished with Danna slamming out of the apartment, and how awful she'd felt. "I told her God loves us so much He warns us, but she didn't want to hear about that. Worst of all," Ginger said, "I feel awful, like I did something wrong."

"You told her about God's love," Mom countered.

"I guess I did."

Her mother added, "Your father should never have left you alone. As for the horoscope, his girlfriend should have accepted your 'no, thanks.' I can imagine how awful you might feel about offending her, especially since she's a grown-up, but do you know what?"

"What?"

Mom smiled at her. "I'm proud of you, Ginger, that's what. I'm proud that you stood firm for Christian principles."

"I—I didn't think of that."

"It's the first time you've really stood up to an unbeliever for what God tells us, isn't it?" Grant asked.

"I guess it is," Ginger said, still surprised that they weren't upset.

Grant said, "I'm proud of you, too." He turned to Grandfather Gabriel. "Why don't you tell us what you think?"

Grandfather smiled at Ginger. "Probably we should begin by looking at both sides of the matter.

First, we can understand that Danna might be angry to hear that what she does is connected with the occult . . . especially from an eleven-year-old girl. On the other hand," he continued, "when someone tries to draw Christians into what we know is wrong, we must make a polite but firm stand, which is just what you did, Ginger. It's a bit like saying no to drugs . . . you might offend whoever is trying to get you involved, but you have to do it anyhow. The important thing is to remain kind but firm."

"I was firm," Ginger reflected, "But I was so surprised that I don't think I was kind enough."

"It's not too late for that, Ginger," Grant said. "I'm sure you'll see Danna again."

"Yeah," Ginger said, swallowing hard. "Maybe I will."

Grandfather said, "What you've already done is to plant a seed in Danna's mind. You told her that God loves us and that He warns us in the Bible not to get involved with astrology." He paused. "I sense that you're concerned about her and your father spiritually."

Ginger nodded.

Grandfather said, "Why don't we pray about that now?"

Ginger bowed her head and, before Grandfather started, she prayed, *Thank You, Lord, for letting me tell Danna, even if it wasn't easy. Thank You for loving me even in the middle of trouble. And thank*

You, thank You, for my new family.

The next morning, Katie phoned to invite Ginger to ride to Sunday school with them, so Ginger didn't have to tell Gram what had happened. In the car, Katie asked, "Did you have a good time with your father?"

"It was okay," Ginger said.

Katie's brown eyes searched hers, then she changed the subject. "Hey, I almost forgot . . . Mom said she'd take us ice-skating at the rink today!"

"All right!" Ginger said.

"All right, okay! We'll have a good day," Katie answered. "Don't I sound like a poet who doesn't know it . . . and my feet show it!"

"You're crazy, Katie Cameron!" Ginger said, and she laughed for what seemed the first time in days.

Katie wobbled her head dizzily. "The crazy daisies will hit the ice!"

Ginger laughed again.

In the front seat, Mrs. Cameron joined in their laughter, then said with her wonderful Georgia accent, "Ah even talked Katie's daddy into skating today. Now what do you young ladies think about that?"

Sounding jolly, Mr. Cameron said, "Ah might be rusty at skating, but a lot of weight has been added, and I'm well padded. How's that for rhyming?"

"Oh, no! We're *all* going crazy!" Katie cried.

Ginger couldn't remember when laughing had felt so good. She guessed that the Camerons must need it themselves. *It's going to be a good day*, she thought. The sun was shining, and its golden light turned the rain-greened hillsides even more beautiful.

At Sunday school, everyone was cheerful. The lesson was about Paul traveling through Greece and telling people about Jesus, and somehow it made Ginger feel all right about her firm stand with Danna. The Bible verse was from the Book of Acts: "Be not afraid, but speak, and hold not thy peace; For I am with thee, and no man shall set on thee to hurt thee." And that made her feel better, too.

Late in the afternoon when Ginger returned home from the ice rink with the Camerons, the lively music still resounding in her head, she felt much better. Ten minutes later, the phone rang.

Joshua called out, "Ginger, it's for you! It's your father, and he sounds mad!"

Ginger swallowed hard and hurried to the family room phone. Nearby in the kitchen, it looked like Mom was sending up a quick prayer.

Ginger picked up the phone. "Hi, Dad."

"Steve," he corrected in a gruff voice. "Steve."

"I'm sorry," she apologized. "Hi . . . Steve."

"That's better," he said, though he didn't sound any more pleased by it. "Your stepbrother was right, I'm mad! From now on, you treat Danna right!"

Ginger gulped again. "I tried to. I really tried to."

"Lay off that Christian stuff," he warned her, "like about not reading horoscopes."

"I only told Danna that God doesn't want us to fool with occult stuff," Ginger protested. "Danna wanted to read it to me, and I just said, 'No, thanks.' Then she asked me why not, and I told her the truth, that God loves us and wants to protect us—"

"That's exactly what I mean," Dad interrupted. "Lay off of it!"

Beside her, Mom said, "I'd like to speak to your father for a minute, please."

Flustered, Ginger handed the phone over to her, not knowing what to expect.

"Hello, Steve," Mom said in a nice, even voice. "This is Sallie. Excuse me for breaking in, but I don't think it's right for you to badger Ginger over something you didn't witness. Can't you imagine the pressure this trouble with your girlfriend is putting on an eleven-year-old girl?"

Dad said something, then Mom continued. "I think the court would take a very dim view of your suddenly insisting upon your visiting rights, bringing Ginger to your apartment, and then leaving her there unsupervised."

Her father talked for awhile, then Mom said, "Thank you for taking such a thoughtful view of the matter. Have a good week, Steve. Good-bye."

Hanging up the phone, she turned to Ginger.

"Your father has given me his word that he won't leave you alone any more on Saturdays. In fact, he'd like to take you to the San Diego Zoo next Saturday if it's not raining. How does that strike you?"

"A lot better," Ginger decided. "You did it just right."

"What's that?" Mom asked.

"Making a firm stand."

Mom smiled. "Thank you. A good thing I prayed," she said. "I hope you're not upset that I interfered."

"You did just what a good mother should."

Mom's blue eyes brightened, and she caught Ginger in a hug. Even though Joshua was watching, it was a warm and comforting moment. With Mom holding her, it seemed to Ginger that nothing in life, not even taking a firm stand, could ever hurt too badly again.

7

Lord, please don't let me have to make a firm stand again today, Ginger prayed as Dad and Danna picked her up the next Saturday morning. As it was, Dad didn't look too happy. Since all three of them didn't fit in his sports car, he had to drive Danna's old yellow clunker. *And, Lord, please show Your love through me to Dad and Danna.*

"Ready for the San Diego Zoo, kiddo?" Dad asked her as they drove away from her house.

"Yup." Ginger settled in the backseat behind Danna and unzipped her green school jacket. "I was only there once a long time ago. I can hardly remember it."

She thought Danna would resent having to go,

but in the front seat, Danna remarked to Dad, "I'm glad to check it out. They're using the zoo for background for lots of fashion shots lately. I might get a job there. You never know."

Ginger decided not to comment, and she gazed out the window. It was a gray morning, but at least it wasn't raining like it had all week. January and February were rainy season, and she hoped it wouldn't rain on any more Saturdays if Dad planned to keep on taking her out.

In San Diego, they drove off the freeway on Park Boulevard. Huge trees towered on the hillsides, and even the bridges were covered with ivy. As they rounded a curve, she saw downtown skyscrapers, then Balboa Park, where Spanish buildings housed museums and theaters.

Dad said, "Some Saturday we'll come to the Space Theater."

Ginger tried to sound enthusiastic. "All right!"

"Maybe by then I'll have moved to L.A.," Danna put in.

No one responded.

After a while Dad said, "Almost to the zoo." They drove by a carousel and a miniature railroad, then into the zoo parking lot. The parking row signs pictured animals and said *Parrot*, *Tiger*, *Rhino*, *Gorilla*, and others. They parked in *Tiger*.

Getting out of the car, Danna darted a mistrustful glance at Ginger and moved to Dad's other side. As they started for the entrance, Ginger noticed that all three of them wore jeans. Dad and Danna wore old matching denim jackets, and Danna sported white boots dotted with silvery spangles.

While Dad bought tickets, Ginger and Danna glanced around at the palm trees and the U.S. and California flags hanging limply from the flagpole. The silence between them was just as limp, Ginger thought. She noticed Danna's dark hair with its golden streaks. "The air's damp," she said to break the silence. "Your hair's going to be ruined."

"Never mind," Danna answered in an even tone. "And don't you make any more trouble for me."

Ginger felt her temper rising, but she said, "I don't plan to. I don't like trouble, either."

Danna raised her chin. "I'll keep that in mind."

It occurred to Ginger that Danna always looked sideways at her, never quite in the eyes.

"Ready, kiddos?" Dad asked. "Let's see the zoo."

Stepping through the turnstiles, Ginger's first glimpse was of pink flamingos standing stilty-legged on the grass in front of their pond. They reminded her of how awkward she usually felt—all knees and elbows. Nearby, beautiful peacocks strutted and preened, reminding her of Danna, who just happened to be applying more bright red lipstick.

Danna said, "Think I'll have a look at the gift shops while you two wander around."

"I'd planned for us to take the bus first," Dad objected, "I thought that way we'd know what we want to see afterwards."

Danna shrugged. "If you say so."

Dad shot her a warning look, then he went over to buy tickets for the double-decker buses. When he returned, they lined up for "upper deck" with other visitors, high on a bridge alongside the aviary.

"Look in here," Ginger said, peering in through the greenery. "That fern looks like it could grab someone."

Dad chuckled. "It sure does."

Nearby, exotic birds peered at her, and Ginger read from their wooden name boards, "Scarlet ibis . . . blue Phillipine gallinule . . . roseate spoonbill. . . ."

Danna remarked, "They'd look good in a modeling shot if they didn't detract attention."

"You wouldn't want that, would you?" Dad taunted.

"Never mind!" she snapped.

They didn't sound very lovey this morning, Ginger decided—not that they ever did. Mom and Grant were the ones who acted lovey, even though they were married.

As they waited in the bus line, there were visitors with babies in strollers and in back carriers. After a while, Danna asked, "When's your mother going to have the kid?"

"Middle of June," Ginger replied, remembering what Danna had said about the baby ruining things for her family. "How come you asked?"

Danna shrugged. "No special reason."

Ginger offered, "The doctor says it's a boy."

"Oh, yeah?" Danna answered.

Glancing at Dad, Ginger decided he didn't want to hear about it.

In front of them, groups of zoo visitors filled the double-decker buses. Their group started forward, but Danna stopped in her tracks. "There's no roof on the upper deck. My hair will get all frizzy. You're not getting me up there."

"It's too late now," Dad pointed out.

"Not for me!" Danna said. "I'm riding below!" She jostled past them and headed through the crowd for the lower deck bus line.

"What if she doesn't get on?" Ginger asked.

Dad urged her forward. "If I know Danna, she'll get on."

"Oh." Ginger stepped onto the bus's upper deck. "Hey, we can get the front seat!" she said, scrambling forward.

She sat down, excited, and noticed Dad watching to make sure Danna got on below.

"She's on." He sat back and ran his fingers through his dark kinky hair, then smoothed his moustache. "That Danna's quite a girl, kiddo."

Ginger said, "I guess so."

At last, the bus started forward, and a voice spoke on the speaker near Ginger. "Good morning, ladies and gentlemen, boys and girls. Welcome to the world-famous San Diego Zoo. I'm your tour guide, and I'll be telling you about the animals as we drive along. To your right, we have the Caribbean flamingos, whose coloration comes from their diet of shrimp and other seafood. . . ."

Ginger sat forward, glancing all around as they rode along by the gift shops' roofs, then the treetops.

The tour guide continued. "To your right, we have Bird and Primate Mesas, where the monkeys swing. To your left, the Children's Petting Zoo. Straight ahead, Reptile Mesa. And coming up, Tiger River."

"All right?" Dad asked Ginger.

She nodded. "Maybe I'll write a report on this for class. Hey, look, there's the tigers! . . . behind the waterfall." It was a beautiful sight. And, in the distance over a giant aviary, the yellow cars of the Skyfari aerial cable lift glided over the green hills and valleys of the zoo.

The bus drove by huge hippos submerged in their concrete pools, then past emus, antelope, sea lions, and even roosters who really crowed "Cock-a-doodle-do!" They drove by Persian leopards and East African warthogs while the tour guide told about them. Best of all was riding along in the treetops and being as high as the giraffes and elephants.

The bus stopped by the brown bears, who stood on their hind legs and stared hopefully at them. The tour guide called out, "Let's wave at Spanky and Sheila."

As people waved, the bears stood on their hind

legs and waved their huge paws. The tour guide threw them treats and said, "Let's see under your feet, Spanky and Sheila!"

To everyone's delight, the bears sat back like big babies and showed off the undersides of their feet. Ginger laughed and applauded with everyone else.

Driving along again, the tour guide said, "Our anteaters are our healthiest animals. Anyone know why?"

Ginger didn't know why, but others guessed all kinds of reasons before the guide quipped, "They have lots of anti-bodies."

"Ahhhh!" everyone groaned, which only made the guide tell more corny jokes.

Ginger darted a grin at her father.

"Having a good time?" he asked.

"Yeah, it's okay."

When the bus trip was over, they met Danna on the street and wandered toward the elephants.

Ginger said, "I rode an elephant at the Wild Animal Park."

"Anyone can take an elephant or even a camel ride," Danna replied, unimpressed. "All you have to do is pay for it."

"No, I was a volunteer in the elephant show," Ginger explained, then was sure Danna didn't believe her. "I really was. You can ask Mom or Grant or any girl in my class."

Danna sniffed. "I know a girl who did a bathing suit modeling layout on an elephant."

Ginger searched for something to say that wouldn't irritate her. "I'll bet you'd look wonderful riding an elephant."

Danna brightened. "Thanks. Maybe I would."

It was nice to be with Dad, Ginger thought as the day continued, but spending time with Danna wasn't too much fun.

The next Saturday they went to a movie, and the next, to a kids' play. By Valentine's Day, Ginger was used to spending Saturdays with Dad and Danna. The one thing she worried about was Danna borrowing a lot of money from Dad so she could buy a new car. Ginger guessed Dad didn't want her to know about it, but Danna had a way of letting out secrets without thinking like suddenly asking, "Can I skip the first month's car payment?" She hoped Danna didn't just like Dad for his money.

The one good thing was, Ginger hadn't had to make any more firm stands that made them mad. Every week she tried to be thoughtful and kind, but about all the three of them actually managed was a shaky truce.

For Valentine's Day, Grant bought Ginger, Joshua, and Lilabet small red heart-shaped boxes of chocolates. And he bought Mom a beautiful blue maternity dress. "To match your blue eyes," he told her.

Mom beamed. "It does look like I should start

wearing maternity clothes. Just this morning the zipper broke on the roomiest skirt I own."

Ginger glanced at her mother's growing waistline. Everyone was beginning to notice. Last Sunday at church a lady had said, "Oh, Sallie, a baby! How wonderful!" Another had asked Ginger, "What do you think about having a baby in the family?"

"It's okay, I guess," she'd replied. She noticed that Joshua had edged away, and she'd felt like it herself. There was something about Mom and Grant having a baby that made her feel uneasy—or maybe the word was threatened.

By mid-March, Ginger was getting used to seeing Mom in maternity clothes, and she even got to feel the baby moving. She'd put her hand on Mom's stomach, and it would be still, then suddenly it'd feel fluttery.

"Just wait a minute," Mom said, "and you'll feel some real kicking. You were a good kicker yourself."

Ginger couldn't imagine it. "Did I hurt you?"

Mom smiled and shook her head. "Never. You were considerate even then."

"Really?" Ginger asked.

Mom nodded. "Really."

Grant said, "Let's hope this little fella is considerate."

"He will be," Mom assured him. "He's going to be just like you, Grant Gabriel."

Grant laughed. "I guess we'd better see about

turning the guest room into a nursery soon." He turned to Joshua. "Think you can give me a hand with painting it next weekend?"

Joshua frowned. "Do I have a choice?"

"Try to lighten up a little, Josh," Grant suggested. "After all, you're going to have a little brother."

Ginger knew what Joshua was thinking. He'd already yelled at her, "Not a brother, a *step*brother, just like you're a *step*sister! We've got too many kids in this family already!"

Lately, he'd been nastier to her than ever, even when she didn't deserve it. She didn't want to tell Mom or Grant. If only she could talk to Grandfather Gabriel, but he'd just moved out to the desert to house-sit for some friends from his old church. She wouldn't see him till they visited there during Easter vacation. When he phoned, he said he'd already made good progress on writing his book.

By the end of March, Grant and Joshua had painted the nursery a pale blue, and Mom had stenciled a white, yellow, and dark blue hot-air balloon on the crib wall. She'd sewn pale blue curtains and bought matching window shades with light outlines of clouds. The fluffy white rug had been cleaned and put back down. Friends had given Mom an old changing table and a chest of drawers, which she'd painted white.

One evening after Grant and Joshua had carried the furniture in, Mom stood back and asked, "Doesn't it look perfect?"

"Yeah," Ginger said. "It looks nice, especially your hot-air balloon. You're really a good artist."

"Why, thank you, Ginger," Mom said. "My art teacher says I'm coming right along. She wants me to show some of my more serious pictures at an exhibition."

Ginger turned to see what Joshua thought, but he was already leaving the room.

Lilabet asked, "Is that baby going to take naps?"

"We certainly hope so," Grant answered.

"I'll read stories to him," Lilabet decided. "That's what I'll do. I'll read lots of stories to him."

Mom hid a smile. "The baby will like that."

Ginger exchanged smiles with Mom and Grant about Lilabet's so-called reading. "You can tell him your own stories too, Lilabet." Lilabet made up crazy stories, stringing her sentences together with "ands" until she'd loudly announce, "The end!"

Lilabet nodded solemnly. "I'll *read* him stories, and I'll *tell* him stories." She turned to Mom and Grant, and asked, "Why doesn't Joshua like our new baby?"

Ginger darted a glance at Grant.

His grayish-blue eyes filled with concern for an instant, then he said, "Josh just isn't used to the idea of a little brother yet. He'll get used to it soon. You'll see."

I hope so, Ginger thought; *I sure do hope so. And I hope I get used to that baby, too!*

8

"No school for a week!" Joshua said as he flopped onto the family room couch with Lilabet, who was watching "Sesame Street."

"A whole week," Ginger marveled as she set the table behind them. In the morning, they'd leave for Anza-Borrego Desert State Park to see the desert in bloom and, as Mom said, "to get away from our usual responsibilities." Ginger just hoped she could get away from her troubles with Joshua.

Grant called in through the back door, "Anyone want to come out to see the surprise for our trip?"

He sounded so excited that Ginger left the silverware in a heap on the table and followed behind Joshua and Lilabet.

Outside, Ginger stopped in amazement. "A minivan!"

Grant laughed and Mom asked, "How's that for a surprise? We turned in my old car and bought the van."

"It's sure an improvement," Ginger said with admiration. Mom's old car had broken down twice last week; besides, lots of kids' parents had minivans. "I'm glad you chose tan."

Grant said, "Mom will soon have four of you to drive around, and we thought this was just right for her now."

Joshua eyed it and started back inside.

Grant asked, "How do you like it, Josh?"

"It's okay, I guess," he answered.

Mom's and Grant's smiles faded, and Ginger quickly put in, "It's super, really super! Won't Grandfather be surprised!"

Joshua glared at her and muttered, "Quit acting."

Ginger hissed, "Do you have to ruin everything?"

He glared harder at her, and Ginger turned in time to hear Mom say, "We thought we'd buy it before our trip to the desert tomorrow morning. Come see the inside."

Lilabet clambered in first, and Ginger climbed in behind her. The interior was tan, too, and the seats and carpet smelled new. The two front seats were widely spaced, and the two middle seats were close together. Three people could easily sit on the backseat. "Seven seats," Ginger said. "Counting Grandfather and the baby, we'll fit in just right."

Lilabet made herself comfortable on the middle seat and announced, "It's a minivan."

"Right, Lilabet, right," Ginger agreed. She grinned at Mom and Grant. "It's going to make the trip perfect."

Mom smiled. "I hope so. Now we'd better get inside and eat dinner so we can finish packing."

Getting out of the van, Ginger felt determined to help make it a good trip. It'd be good to get a rest from school and from a Saturday with Dad and Danna. She hoped Joshua would lighten up, so they'd have a rest from his grouchiness.

The next morning, they pulled onto the freeway at nine o'clock, suitcases strapped to the roof rack. Mom and Grant sat in front, Ginger and Lilabet in the middle seat, and Joshua had the whole backseat to grouch to himself.

An hour later, they drove out into the green foothills of the Laguna Mountains. The road curved through pine trees and barren ridges, then wound down the other side, where white stalks of yucca bloomed on the rugged hillsides.

After a long time Grant said, "There it is . . . below in the distance . . . the Anza-Borrego Desert."

Lilabet peered out and asked, "Where's Grandfather?"

Everyone laughed. There were nothing but hillsides with cactus and huge granite boulders, then the flat desert below.

Gazing through her window, Ginger said, "It looks like a place for cowboy movies. But I don't think even cowboys could ride through some of these hills. There are too many prickly plants . . . and boulders for Indians to hide behind."

"I can't wait to start painting," Mom said. "There's such an ethereal beauty to the desert, even if some people do call it a wrinkled wasteland or a lunar landscape. And just look at that brilliant blue sky and those puffy white clouds."

"I wouldn't want to live here in the summer," Joshua said. "It gets over 120 degrees!" Last fall he had visited the Willets' home, where they'd be staying with Grandfather, and had written a class report about Anza-Borrego. All week he'd been acting like he knew everything about deserts.

"Why don't you tell us about Anza-Borrego, Josh?" Grant suggested. "I could use a refresher course myself. For example, where did it get that name?"

Sounding pleased, Joshua explained, "Anza was a Spanish explorer and, almost a hundred years before California became a state, he led people through here from Mexico. Borrego is the Spanish name for the desert bighorn sheep that live in the mountains. It's the biggest state park in our country."

"And it's one of California's last untamed frontiers," Grant added.

"It looks like it," Ginger said, though she rather liked its eeriness. "What are all those tall, prickly, stick plants? Look, they're blooming with little red flags!"

Joshua said, "That's octotillo."

"And there's cactus in bloom," Mom marveled. "It's been such a long time since I've been in a desert after rainy season that I'd forgotten how beautiful it can be."

"Then I'm doubly glad I brought you," Grant said, keeping his eyes on the curving road. "Springtime in the desert reminds me of spiritual rebirth. Even the harshest-looking plants give birth to delicate blossoms."

Ginger wondered if he meant her spiritual rebirth—her accepting the Lord—though at times she still was prickly. Not as prickly as Joshua was lately, though.

As they drove down into the valley, miles of rose and yellow wildflowers brightened the desert. Grandfather told them there'd be palm canyons and a waterfall and old Indian ruins, too, so it sounded like lots of good exploring ahead.

After a while, they drove past concrete block houses, some with foil on the windows to keep out the sun. Ginger said, "I hope the Willet house doesn't have foil on the windows."

"Of course it doesn't," Joshua said in a belittling tone.

"We shouldn't be too far from the Willets' house

now," Grant said. "Josh, could you keep an eye out—"

"I think that's the road!" Joshua said.

Minutes later, they pulled up in the gravel driveway of a white concrete block house. Grant honked the horn, and then Grandfather was hurrying out, shading his eyes against the sun to be sure it was them in the minivan. His mouth opened wide in surprised recognition, then he beamed and waved.

As soon as they opened the doors, hot, dry desert air hit them. "Wow, it's hot!" Ginger said with the rest of them.

Grandfather laughed, then they were talking and hugging. "I finished writing the book," he said, "but how I've missed every single one of you!" Hugging him, Ginger knew it was true. He added, "I've even got everything ready for lunch."

"Gourmet fare?" Grant teased.

"Sandwiches on paper plates!" Grandfather answered. "Come in out of the noonday heat. We can explore after lunch."

Ginger lugged her suitcase into the house, glad for the cool, air-conditioned air. The concrete block walls were painted stark white, but it was a comfortable place with no foil on the windows. Instead, there were lots of shades and heavily lined white drapes. She felt excited, even if she did have to share a room with Lilabet.

At lunch Grandfather said, "Let's keep meals

simple here, so we're free of cooking and cleaning up afterward."

"It sounds good to me," Mom said. "I'm getting so clumsy that it takes me forever to get anything done."

Grandfather said, "It does appear that baby's growing. I think you look just as God intended mothers to look—wonderful."

After lunch, they drove out to explore in the minivan. After a while, the road circled around, and Grandfather said, "This is Christmas Circle, where Juan Anza and the settlers passed through in 1775. Can you imagine trekking through this land on foot and horseback in those days?"

"What an adventure it must have been," Grant remarked.

Ginger could imagine the settlers in her mind's eye—horses and mules and straggly lines of people moving through the mountains, then across this desert to the mountains on the other side. "I wish I could have been there," she said.

"Some of them died," Grandfather responded. "The desert's a harsh place to travel, even now. One has to use good sense."

Joshua said, "Then we'd better keep an eye on Ginger. She doesn't have much sense."

"Josh, that's not true," Grant objected.

Ginger turned to Joshua and snapped, "So there!"

He looked out his window, ignoring her.

A sign said, *Visitors' Center*, but when they drove

in, Ginger saw no sign of buildings. Ghostly green palo verde trees abloom with yellow flowers surrounded the parking lot; beyond, there was only the glare of sunshine on the desert. They climbed out of the minivan into the fierce heat, and Grandfather said, "Follow me."

He led them past prickly plants, many of them in bloom, with metal markers showing names like fiery duster, bladderpod, beavertail cactus, buckhorn cholla, and honey mesquite. Finally they saw the underground Visitors' Center, which was built of tan rocks and blended into the hillside. "Water faucet's there," Grandfather said. "It's good water, too. I can't get enough of it myself."

"I'm dying of thirst!" Ginger yelled and raced to the faucet. She drank and drank the cold water. Finally, she felt better. Wiping her face, she hurried into the Visitors' Center.

After the bright glaring sunshine, it seemed dark inside. Once her eyes had adjusted, she saw books, postcards, and colorful exhibits, including a big display map of places to visit.

The others had followed her in, and Lilabet jumped up and down. "I wanna push the button! I wanna push the button!"

Grant said, "Go ahead, Lilabet."

She pushed it, and a tiny light came on the display map at Pina Spring, then at Split Mountain, then Borrego Palm Canyon.

Behind her, Grandfather said, "We can go there,

to Borrego Palm Canyon, for an outdoor worship service tomorrow morning."

"You mean they have church outdoors here?" Ginger asked.

Joshua jibed, "You mean you've never heard of outdoor services, like for Easter?"

"Sure," Ginger returned, not that she'd ever been to one.

Grandfather said, "This one meets every Sunday this time of year. That's where I've been attending church."

Ginger felt like telling Joshua, *See, you're not so smart!* but the announcer said, "Two minutes until the show starts."

In the small, darkened theater, a slide presentation showed Anza-Borrego. As the beautiful slides flashed before them, the narrator spoke of "bleak desolate wastelands where distances are deceptive and humans seem insignificant . . . plants you wouldn't want to touch and animals you wouldn't want to be touched by. But it's a special kind of beauty, a magnificent dryness from the sunbaked flats to the pine-covered mountains."

The next day when Ginger opened her bedroom drapes, she already felt at home in the desert. "Sunday morning," she told Lilabet. "You know what? We're going to church outside!"

"Outside?" Lilabet repeated, rubbing her eyes. Her blonde hair, usually a neat cap, was unruly and wild.

Ginger almost laughed as she nodded. "Outside."

When they arrived at the Borrego Palm Canyon Campground for the service, Ginger sat down between Mom and Grandfather Gabriel on a half-filled semicircle of bleachers. Fortunately Joshua sat beside Grant, farthest away.

Campers arrived quietly from all around, and a morning breeze stirred the warm air. Nearby, a jackrabbit peered at them through the brush. Yellow and rose wildflowers bloomed across the stark desert, and white yucca flowers marched up the nearby mountains. A hush filled the air, making Ginger feel wonderfully close to God.

A minister stepped forward into the silence. "Shall we stand and sing 'Morning Has Broken'?"

Their voices sounded pure as the words about "the first morning" and "the first bird" filled the soft desert air. After a while, the minister spoke about God's love, and birds twittered from the nearby scrub. It was perfect to worship outdoors, Ginger decided. Perfectly wonderful.

Later, as the service ended, they all stood again in the midst of the desert and mountains and sang "How Great Thou Art." Ginger sang with all of her might, "O Lord my God, when I in awesome wonder consider all the worlds Thy hands have made. . . ."

Afterwards, they took the self-guided trail to Borrego Palm Canyon, walking slowly so Mom could keep up. Her middle was so big that it took her forever to do things, making her laugh a lot. When they finally reached the end of the rocky canyon, there were not only wildflowers abloom all around them, but a grove of palm trees, a cool stream, and a waterfall.

"An oasis," Ginger marveled. "They *are* real, not just something you read about in books." If only there could be an oasis of peace between herself and Joshua.

The next day, they explored Indian ruins: sweat houses for health cures, shelter caves still black with smoke, pictures cut into stone, and boulders worn into *metates* in which Indian women once ground their corn.

Grandfather said, "Indian women picked these cat's claw pods for dinner, and they used those indigo bushes for dyes. Standing here, can't you imagine the Indian men and boys returning from a hunt with an antelope on their shoulders?"

"Yeah . . . I really can," Ginger answered.

Joshua muttered, "I'll bet," and gave her a don't-be-ridiculous look.

She turned away quickly. She tried to put his testiness out of mind as they wandered beyond graceful smoke trees in the washes. She tried to keep him out of sight as they stopped to admire a barrel cactus's bright yellow flowers and the orchid-colored blooms on beavertail cactus. Yet he was always the first to yell, "Hey, look at that lizard!" or to see the rabbits that bounded through the brush.

Every day Mom painted the places they visited: Elephant Trees, Lookout Point, Borrego Badlands, Scissors Crossing, and Yaqui Well. Her painting them made everything all the more interesting, and there were exciting tales, too, of lost ships, gold mines, and strange old prospectors like Peg Leg Smith.

Every day, when the sun and the shadows were just right, Ginger gazed at a rock scar on the mountains that looked like an angel. Every night, when they sat outside to enjoy the cool air, she gazed at the velvety black sky bright with stars. It seemed she saw galaxies beyond distant galaxies, then galaxies beyond. Not that she'd say so in front of Joshua.

The last day, Grandfather took her to lunch at an old hotel, La Casa del Zorro. After they'd ordered, the two of them sat in the elegant Butterfield Station dining room and admired oil paintings of Butterfield Overland stagecoaches traveling through nearby places years ago.

"I'm glad you love the desert," he said. "I suppose you don't feel like leaving, either."

"It's been one of the best weeks of my life," she answered, "except for Joshua bugging me."

"I'm sorry he's always after you lately," Grandfather said. "Why do you suppose that is?"

Ginger shrugged. "I don't know." She smoothed the white cloth napkin on her lap. "Before Mom and Grant got married, I thought he'd like me more.

Then we moved in, and . . . I know he likes Mom, but he doesn't like me at all."

"Do you suppose he's jealous?" Grandfather asked.

She looked up. "Jealous? You mean jealous of me?"

Grandfather took a roll from the basket and began to butter it. "Joshua used to have Grant and Lilabet and me all to himself. When you and your mother came, he had to share us, just like you have to share your mother."

"I guess so," Ginger said, beginning to understand. Sometimes she didn't like to share Mom at all. "But why would he be getting worse and worse lately? . . . especially now, when Mom's going to have a baby?"

"Let's look at it this way," Grandfather said. "When you put a new chicken in a coop, all of the other chickens flutter around, upset . . . until they get used to it. When you and your mother moved in, it was like that for Joshua . . . and now, just when he's getting used to that, there's another chick on the way. He's unsettled and a little jealous."

"But what can I do about it?" Ginger asked.

Grandfather answered, "You need to love him."

"I have to love him?" she repeated. "Sometimes I don't even like him."

Grandfather said, "When someone becomes jealous, they often become full of anger and resentment, and that's probably where Joshua is now." He smiled at her. “But love casts out jealousy and anger.”

It sounds complicated, Ginger thought. Then the waiter came bringing their taco salads. She’d have to think about it . . . about love and jealousy and anger and resentment . . . though she couldn’t imagine what good it would do. Still, what an amazing idea . . . that Joshua was jealous of her and that she had to love him.

9

The Saturday after Easter, Dad and Danna picked Ginger up in Danna's new car. "I only have a few hours to spend with you, kiddo," he explained to Ginger. He managed a small smile under his moustache. "Things are messed up at work."

Ginger buckled up in the backseat. "It's okay."

"How was your week at Anza-Borrego?" he asked as they drove off. He sounded like he was trying to make polite conversation, but Ginger suspected it was more than that. He wanted to know about her . . . and about Mom.

"Nice," Ginger said, deciding not to tell too much. She gave her gum a loud crack. "I had a wonderful time."

"Good," Dad replied, then didn't ask anything else.

Anza-Borrego had taken them away from responsibilities for a while, but it hadn't stopped their problems, Ginger thought. Joshua resented her. And he didn't like Mom and Grant having a baby—nor did she sometimes. As if that weren't bad enough, she still didn't like being with Dad and Danna, either.

As Dad drove along, Danna remarked, "I was hoping we'd stop at Contempo Furniture. They're having a fabulous sale, and I can't stand my old couch one more day."

"I thought you couldn't afford new furniture," Dad said.

"Well, I can afford a down payment," she replied huffily.

"You haven't made one car payment," Dad complained. "If you can make a couch down payment, you can just pay me."

Danna batted her lashes at him. "If you don't trust me, maybe I should take that job offer in L.A.! At least, it might turn into something more important than I have here."

Ginger gazed out the window, hoping Danna wouldn't get the better of Dad. But the next thing she knew he was saying, "Okay, we'll stop to look at couches, but don't count on getting any more loans from me."

While Dad and Danna argued on, Ginger

prayed, *God, I know Dad's not perfect, but I'm afraid Danna likes him mostly for his money. Can't you make him see that? And can't You stop them from dating somehow?*

Later, at the furniture store, it appeared that her prayer wasn't going to be answered, because Danna bought a white curved couch. "Just the kind I've been dreaming about," she gushed to Dad. "I'm so glad you understand. I'll make the car payment next month . . . I promise."

"I sure hope so," he answered stiffly.

"Don't count on it," Ginger muttered under her breath.

The stop at Contempo Furniture had taken so long there was only time for a fast food hamburger. The next thing Ginger knew, Dad was driving her back home. "How's your mother feeling, kiddo?" he asked.

"Fine," she replied and chewed her gum hard.

"That new baby will be here in a few months," he continued, "before we even know it."

"Yeah, I guess so."

Danna said to him, "You sure are curious about your ex-wife lately. Every time we're out with Ginger, you ask about her. And when we drive up to their house, you're always looking around like you hope to see her."

"What's wrong with that?" Dad inquired.

Danna drew a deep breath. "Since you asked, I think her getting married and having a kid has really thrown you. I think you're jealous, or at least resentful!"

"You're crazy," Dad flung back. "Besides that, it's none of your business."

"Well," Danna said, "you asked."

Ginger was glad to get home. "Thanks a lot," she told Dad as she climbed out of the car.

"Sure . . . see you next Saturday, kiddo."

"Yeah."

In the house, Mom was just coming out of her bedroom, blinking her blue eyes awake. She smiled guiltily. "I was so tired, I had to take a nap. You're home early. Did you have a good visit?"

"It was okay. Dad had to go to work."

"On Saturday afternoon?"

Ginger nodded. "He says things are a mess at work."

"I'm sorry to hear that," Mom said. "Everything seemed to be going well for him at last."

It was strange that they still cared about each other even though they were divorced, Ginger thought. She remembered when she'd wanted them to get married again, even imagined it, but it was too late for that. Besides, she liked Grant a lot, and Mom was happy now.

"Grant and I are running down to the mall to look at strollers," Mom told her. "Want to come along?"

"Can't," Ginger answered. "Too much homework."

Mom was forever thinking about that baby, maybe because her middle was getting so big, Ginger decided. You could feel the baby kick harder now, and that made it more interesting. She wondered why Joshua refused to feel it. He wouldn't even look at Mom's middle. As Ginger headed for her room, she remembered the trouble he'd gotten into the night before, when he showed up late for dinner. It seemed he was in trouble a lot lately and getting grouchier than ever.

The rest of April zoomed by, then May. With so much happening at the end of the school year, some days Ginger could scarcely remember what came next. Already Joshua was signed up for camp the week after school let out. Grandfather mentioned that Gabriel cousins from northern California might have an extra room during their vacation at Yosemite.

"If so," he asked Ginger, "would you like to go?"

She'd never been there, and lots of the kids at school went to Yosemite. "If you're going," she decided.

Every day Mom's middle seemed more huge, and the nursery was ready for the baby. Mom had even packed a small suitcase for the hospital. "Just in case it's early," she told Ginger. "You were born early."

"I was?" Ginger asked.

Mom laughed. "You mean you don't remember?"

One night at dinner Grant said, "The first Saturday in June, I'm taking all three of you to a sibling class at the hospital, so you'll know what to expect when we have the baby."

Lilabet's brown eyes narrowed. "What's that?"

"Sibling means a sister or brother," Grant explained. "You and Joshua and Ginger are siblings. This new baby will be your sibling, too."

"Oh," Lilabet said. "I thought he'd be a baby brother."

Ginger tried not to laugh, and Grant said with a straight face, "Maybe we'd better just call it baby brother class."

"No," Lilabet responded, "let's call it sibling class."

"Then sibling class it is," Grant said.

Mom said, "They'll show you the hospital rooms, even the nursery with all of the babies in it."

"I guess that'll be interesting," Ginger decided.

Joshua grumbled, "Do I *have* to go?"

"I'd think that you of all people would want to go, since you're going to have a brother," Grant said. "I can't wait to have another male member of this family myself!"

Mom and Ginger laughed, but not Joshua.

The last week of school, she and Joshua won honor roll trips to the San Diego Zoo, but he didn't even enjoy that—and he hadn't been to the zoo in ages.

Finally school was out and everyone was yelling,

"Have a good summer! Have a good vacation!"

"You, too!" Ginger answered. It seemed that she'd just started at Santa Rosita Christian a short time ago. Yet it seemed that she'd been going there forever, too. It really felt like her school now.

That night she phoned Dad. "I forgot to tell you. I have to go to a sibling class at the hospital tomorrow morning."

He sounded almost as grumpy as Joshua, but he said, "It's okay, kiddo. I should work tomorrow anyhow. How's Mom now?"

"Fine," Ginger replied, "except she's tired."

His tone became thoughtful. "She was tired before you were born, too. I guess it's heavy work, carrying a baby around."

The next day, while Mom slept in, Grant took them to the hospital. The sibling class met in a school-like classroom with kids of all ages and a few parents, too.

The teacher, Miss Davies, was bubbly and enthusiastic, and wore a flowery dress that matched the mauve-colored walls.

"You're all going to have a wonderful adventure," she said. "Each of you in this room is going to have a new baby at home soon. In this class we tell you what to expect. We even tell you how to hold a baby and feed it with a bottle."

Beside Ginger, Joshua muttered, "Not me. I'm not holding any baby."

She ignored him. She felt upset sometimes, too, about Mom having this baby, but right now she wanted to know more about how Mom would do it—and that she'd be okay.

Miss Davies said, "First, we'll show a film about birthing. You might want to imagine the lady in it as your mother."

The lights went off, and the film began with a mother arriving at the hospital. They took her to a birthing room, where she changed into a delivery gown. Her husband and other children stayed with her and helped her breathe right. She had to push hard to get the baby out.

Suddenly a doctor held a brand-new baby. He cleaned and weighed it, then gave the baby to the mother. Later, the film showed the baby in the hospital nursery with other babies. Last, they showed how to hold a baby and give it a bottle.

When the film ended and the lights went on again, Ginger asked Grant, "Are we going to be at the hospital, too?"

"Every family does that differently," he answered. "Mom doesn't want a large audience, so just I'll be going with her."

"Oh." Ginger felt a little disappointed, but relieved, too.

Miss Davies said, "We're going to have a tour of obstetrics now. That's the special place in a hospital for mothers and babies. Your mother will probably stay here for a few days. And now here's a surprise.

We're all going to dress like doctors and nurses." She passed out green paper pants and shirts in all sizes, then white paper shower caps, slippers, and gloves, and told how to wear them.

As Ginger put on her crinkling paper outfit, she guessed Joshua was only doing it because everyone else did. Anyhow, kids and parents laughed at how odd they looked in their outfits. She and Grant helped Lilabet into hers, gathering her blonde hair up under the cap. Finished dressing, they laughed at themselves and each other again.

Before long, they shuffled down the hallway in their paper slippers to tour the obstetrics department. It was interesting to see real rooms with tiny-flowered wallpaper like the one Mom would be in.

The tour ended in the hallway, and Miss Davies asked, "Are there any questions?"

Lilabet piped up, "When do we bring that baby back here?"

Others laughed, but Miss Davies turned to Lilabet in all seriousness. "That's a very important question. Your family will keep the baby. It will belong to your family forever."

Forever, Ginger's mind repeated. She felt as worried about that as Lilabet looked now. *Forever was a long time.* Forever and ever and ever.

She and Lilabet decided to wear their paper outfits home, even if people did stare at them on the freeway. When they arrived at the house, Raffles barked loudly at them.

Inside, Mom was cooking spaghetti sauce, and the whole house smelled inviting and homelike. "Well, look at your outfits!" she laughed. "I won't even need a hospital with so many doctors and nurses around. How was the class?"

"Perfect," Grant said. "And how are you?"

"Making sure you won't starve while I'm at the hospital. I've made enough spaghetti sauce for an army. By the way," she added, "it's time to go to the hospital now."

"You're kidding!" Grant said. "It's two weeks early—"

Mom shook her head slowly, her dimples deepening. "It's time to go anyhow."

Grant must have swallowed hard, because his Adam's apple bobbed in his neck. "You're sure? Did you call Dr. Halstead?"

"Just a few minutes ago," Mom said. "He told me to go straight to the hospital and let someone else finish making the spaghetti sauce."

Ginger felt her eyes widening. "You're really going now?"

"If someone will finish the spaghetti—"

"Forget the spaghetti!" Grant interrupted. "Let's go! Ginger, run get your mother's hospital case, then take charge of dinner. Josh, run get your grandfather. He'll take over here."

Mom laughed at him. "Stay calm, dear," she said, then clutched her middle. "Oh, we'd better go!"

Lilabet piped, "Maybe you'll get that baby here!"

"I prefer the hospital!" Grant answered, urgently propelling Mom toward the door.

Raffles woofed and managed to get right in the way as everyone rushed about. Then Grant was helping Mom out the door.

Ginger ran and grabbed Mom's little suitcase from the nursery. Through the window, she saw Joshua trudging along in the backyard toward the guest house. He wasn't even in a hurry!

As she watched, he picked up a rock and turned, fury boiling on his face. Lifting his arm, he threw the rock with all of his might toward the house . . . toward her room! Her mouth fell open as the rock crashed through her window.

Shocked, she felt as if he'd thrown the rock at her. Did he hate her that much?

Suddenly she noticed Mom's suitcase in her hand, and she rushed out and down the hallway. She couldn't tell Mom or Grant! No, she couldn't tell them now. Probably they hadn't heard the rock crash through her window if the car was running.

She ran outside, and Grant's car was indeed running. It was halfway down the drive. "Here it is! Here's your hospital suitcase!" Ginger yelled. She raced after them with Lilabet behind her yelling and Raffles barking.

Grant backed the car up fast. "I forgot!"

Ginger opened the back door and set the suitcase in.

"Thanks!" Mom said, then called back as they

took off again. "I turned off the spaghetti sauce! Take good care of Lilabet!"

Ginger grabbed Lilabet's hand, and she didn't even object. As they stood there, Ginger was scarcely aware of the car driving away; instead, she still saw the fury on Joshua's face.

"They're gonna get that baby now," Lilabet said.

"Yeah," Ginger answered. "Yeah, they sure are."

Nothing would ever be the same again, she thought. Already that baby had changed things for everyone.

10

When the phone rang that afternoon, Grandfather Gabriel answered it in the family room. He'd been expecting a long-distance call, and he listened intently, then beamed at Ginger, Lilabet, and Joshua. "It's Grant! Our new baby's here! Baby and mother are doing fine!"

"Yea!" Ginger cheered, feeling relieved and crazy. "Yea!" she yelled again with Lilabet. "Yea, Mom! Yea, baby!"

Even Raffles stood up and wagged his rear end, but Joshua just turned a dull look on them. Grandfather had just quizzed him about the window, and he hadn't said much about that, either.

"Thanks, Grant, for letting us know," Grandfather said into the phone. "Yes, everything's under control here."

Now everything was under control, Ginger thought and patted Raffles' head. Grandfather had phoned a carpenter friend who would replace the broken windowpane in her room. It was a good thing that the house had old-fashioned windows with little panes, or the damage would have been worse. It was terrible enough to see how much Joshua hated her.

When Grandfather hung up the phone, Joshua asked, "May I go to my room now?"

"We haven't finished this discussion, Josh," Grandfather replied. "We need to talk about God, not the broken window, which is only a symptom of your anger. If we keep God first in our lives, we'll have His love for each other. If we put ourselves first, that love soon disappears. It's God's love that keeps a family in harmony."

He paused. "Josh, you can't just shatter our family like you shattered that window. At the very least, you need to ask Ginger's forgiveness."

Joshua didn't meet her gaze, and his voice was still angry. "I'm sorry."

Grandfather said, "You certainly don't sound like it. Aren't you the least bit sorry?"

This time Joshua sounded regretful. "I'm sorry."

"It's okay," Ginger answered. "I guess you don't like things to change, either. Like me moving here, and now a baby."

He shrugged, his eyes almost closed.

She recalled Grandfather discussing love and jealousy and anger and resentment when they'd eaten lunch at Anza-Borrego. It'd been confusing then, but now she knew what God wanted her to do. She said, "I forgive you for breaking the window, Josh." It wasn't easy, but she made herself go on, "Maybe I don't always act like it, but deep inside, I—I love you."

Joshua's brown eyes opened wide with amazement.

Grandfather nodded approvingly and said, "Now, let's put that behind us. How about celebrating the birth of our new baby with some chocolate cookies and lemonade?"

"Okay," Lilabet said, then turned to wag her finger at Joshua. "Joshua, don't you be bad no more." She headed for the kitchen. "Anyhow, I like chocolate cookies."

"You like any kind of cookies," Ginger said.

Even Joshua had to smile a little at that.

Grandfather said, "Grant will be home for dinner for some of that spaghetti sauce you finished making, Ginger. After dinner, we'll visit your mother and the baby at the hospital. We can pick roses from the garden to take with us."

"Did they decide on the baby's name yet?" she asked.

"Grant said they'd tell us tonight," Grandfather answered. "I think they're being mysterious."

Joshua quietly asked to take cookies to his room, and the rest of them sat down at the family room table, talking about the new baby. Ginger had just bitten into her first cookie when the phone rang again. Grandfather answered it.

"Ginger, it's for you."

It'll be Katie, Ginger thought. Grabbing the telephone, she exclaimed, "Mom had the baby this afternoon!"

Silence filled her ear. "Hello, are you there?"

Dad said in a strained voice, "Congratulations."

Ginger faltered. "I—I thought it'd be Katie."

"It's all right," he said. "I . . . I'm glad to know. Is everything okay?"

Ginger knew he meant Mom. "Yeah, they're all right."

"I'm glad to hear it. Actually, I called to ask how the sibling class went." He hesitated. "And I guess I was missing you today . . . and feeling lonely here in the office."

"Lonely?" she repeated.

"Danna and I broke up," he explained. "She's moving to L.A. next week. You know, she wants to do more modeling."

"I prayed that—" Ginger stopped. She'd better not tell him she'd asked God to stop their dating.

Dad said, "Even though you two didn't start out very well, she ended up thinking you were all right. I'm supposed to tell you she hopes you'll be right about when the baby comes."

Ginger remembered Danna's warning about what trouble a baby could cause in a family. "I guess I'm glad to hear that."

"The rest didn't turn out so good, kiddo," he said. "I'm getting her car since she didn't make payments, and I'm selling my sports car to raise money. Things are bad at Santa Rosita Surfboards lately. I'm moving to a cheaper apartment, too."

"I'm sorry. I really am."

"I'm sorry about a lot of things, too," he remarked. "One thing I'm not sorry about though, and that's . . . having you."

She gripped the phone harder. "Honest?"

"Honest."

He'd always told her he didn't like that kind of talk, but now he'd started it himself. Suddenly she knew she should say the same words to him that God had led her to tell Joshua, even though she was half-scared to do it again. "Hey, you know what?"

"What?"

"I love you."

His voice sounded strangled. "I . . . ah, thanks, kiddo. Even if I never do tell you . . . I love you, too."

Ginger swallowed hard. He loved her, he really did.

While that was soaking in, he added, "Something else, kiddo. Danna was right about one thing. I've been a little resentful about your new life, and now the baby. I guess I still care a lot . . . in a friendly kind of way, about your mother, too."

Relief surged through Ginger, but she tried to sound calm. "I'm glad. I'm really glad." It wasn't easy to discuss this kind of stuff with divorced parents, but she sure felt better to know he cared about them. "Anyhow," she said, "she cares about you, too, in a friendly kind of way."

Grant arrived in time to say grace before dinner, and his praise and thanksgiving lifted all of their spirits. After their "Amen" he said, "I picked up flowers for Mom. We can take them to her when we go after dinner."

Ginger said, "We picked roses for her, too, all colors."

"Good," Grant replied. "We'll fill her room with flowers. And just wait till you see that baby!"

"Who does he look like?" Grandfather asked.

Grant eyed each of them and laughed. "Mostly like himself, except he has dimples like Mom. He has blue eyes, too."

"I hope he doesn't have red hair," Ginger put in.

Grant laughed. "What little he has is brownish."

Blue eyes and brown hair, Ginger thought enviously as she twirled a forkful of spaghetti. "What's his name?"

Grant chuckled. "Be patient. We'll tell at the hospital."

"Well, then," Grandfather said, "we'd better eat fast so we don't die of suspense."

"We'll all have to clean up so that baby doesn't think he has a family of slobs," Grant warned with a grin.

Joshua didn't say anything; he just ate his spaghetti and salad and garlic bread.

Please, God, Ginger prayed, *don't let Joshua stay so mad and don't let him—and the rest of us—be jealous!*

It was almost seven o'clock when they arrived at the hospital. They'd all bathed and changed, Ginger into her new white sundress, and they looked like a shiny family as they walked down the hallway to Mom's room. Ginger held the vaseful of roses carefully so the water wouldn't slosh out. Grant carried his bouquet of mixed flowers, and Lilabet brought a homemade card that she claimed showed Mom in bed with a baby.

"Straight ahead to her room," Grant directed as their shoes tapped on the shiny white floor.

Ginger followed, nervous and excited. What if things went wrong . . . especially with Joshua? She recalled the anger on his face when he'd thrown the rock at her window. Glancing at him now, he seemed more quiet than angry, but you never knew.

Rounding a corner, Grant said, "Second door on the right."

They stepped into the room.

Mom lay in bed, her beautiful brownish-red hair spread across a pillow. She looked tired, but when she saw them, she beamed and her blue eyes sparkled with pleasure. And there, just like in Lilabet's card, lay a tiny baby sleeping next to her. For an instant, Ginger felt jealous . . . yes, jealous . . . green, green, green.

Mom said, "I was hoping you'd come now."

"You couldn't have kept us away," Grant answered, setting his vase of flowers on the stand beside her bed. He bent over her carefully and kissed her forehead.

Everyone else greeted her sort of stiffly and, for an instant, they all seemed like strangers.

"What beautiful flowers," Mom said. "And even roses from the garden to remind me of home. Thank you so much."

Ginger wanted to kiss her, but decided it might disturb the baby. Everyone looked like they didn't know what to do next. Finally she put the roses on the nightstand, too.

"What do you think of your brother?" Mom asked, turning to admire him. "Isn't he a dear little fellow?"

Ginger didn't know what to answer. You couldn't see much of him since he wore a white gown and was wrapped in a white blanket. Only his head and his hands were out. His face was red like they'd warned in the sibling class. Trying not to sound jealous she said, "He sure is little."

Mom smiled. "He weighs exactly what you did at birth . . . eight pounds, eight ounces."

"Really?" Ginger asked.

"Really," her mother answered. "He'll be as big as you are far too soon."

Ginger eyed him more closely. His hair was brown like Grant had told them, and he had fat chipmunk cheeks.

Lilabet peered over Mom at him. "Where's his bottle?"

"He's not drinking from a bottle yet," Mom answered. "He's just getting used to being out here in the world."

Grandfather said, "He reminds me a little of Grant when he was a baby. A nicely shaped head."

"I thought so, too," Mom answered.

Ginger glanced from the baby to Grant and saw no resemblance. Anyhow, Grant's head was mostly covered with hair.

Lilabet held out her homemade card to Mom. "I made it for you." She pointed at the squiggles. "It says, 'We ate chocolate cookies, and we drank lemonade, and we ate spaghetti, and we picked flowers for you . . . and please come home from this hospital soon!' "

Ginger let out a relieved breath. Knowing Lilabet, she might have added, ". . . and Joshua broke Ginger's window!"

"Thank you, Lilabet." After admiring the card, Mom asked Grant to set it on the nightstand with the flowers. "Well, Joshua," she said, turning to him, "what do you think of your brother?"

Joshua glanced down as if to hide his jealousy. "He's all right, I guess."

From the corner of her eye, Ginger saw Dr. Halstead arriving. A good thing, too, because he was an old friend of Grandfather's, and he knew how to fill silences.

Dr. Halstead smiled and shook hands heartily with each of them. "Matthew," he said to Grandfather, "It looks like you've got yourself another grandson."

"That I have," Grandfather said. "I was just counting our blessings. God has worked things out so wonderfully for Sallie and Grant, and through them, for me, too."

Dr. Halstead patted Grandfather's shoulder, then looked at the baby. "This baby seems to know he has visitors; he's waking up. Would you like to hold him, Lilabet?"

Lilabet raised her chin uncertainly, then nodded.

"You sit here on Mom's bed, and we'll get you ready."

Mom moved aside slightly, making more room as Lilabet sat down with her on the bed. Then Dr. Halstead placed a pillow on Lilabet's lap. "Ready?" he asked.

Lilabet nodded, not saying a word.

Dr. Halstead lifted the baby onto Lilabet's pillow and showed her how to hold him. "Now, Lilabet, what do you think?"

Lilabet looked up at him, and she announced

with pride and bewilderment all mixed up with wonder, "This is my little brother."

Mom blinked hard, and Dr. Halstead smiled. "That he is."

After a while Dr. Halstead asked, "How about you, Joshua, you want to hold your brother?"

Joshua shrugged as if he had no choice, then exchanged places with Lilabet and put the pillow on his lap.

"Here you are, Josh," Dr. Halstead said and put the baby on the pillow again. "Have they told you what his name is?"

Joshua shook his head, his eyes darting to Ginger.

Maybe he expected her to make fun of him, she thought. She smiled at him reassuringly.

Mom said, "This seems a perfect time to announce his name. Why don't you do that, Grant?"

In his nice, deep voice Grant announced, "We've named this baby in honor of his grandfather and his brother. His name is Matthew Joshua."

"Why, thank you," Grandfather said, beaming. "Thank you! I'm greatly honored."

Ginger turned to Joshua and saw he was blinking hard even though he was looking at the baby. "Thanks," he said, his voice shaky. "I sure don't deserve it, but I'm—I'm asking . . . I'm asking the Lord to help me do better . . . to not be so jealous and resentful . . . to let His love shine through me more . . . like Ginger."

Tears burst to Ginger's eyes, and she closed them

with thankfulness. *Thank You, thank You, Lord.*

Joshua finished, "Anyhow, thanks a lot for giving . . . for giving him my name, too."

Mom blinked hard again, and Grant said, "Josh, it's an honor for your little brother to have your name. We hope that he'll grow up to be a fine young man like you."

Lilabet said, "Joshua wants to be good now."

"Yes, Lilabet," Grant said, "I think he does."

Even Joshua smiled at Lilabet's explanation, then Dr. Halstead said, "Ginger, how about holding Matthew Joshua Gabriel?"

She sniffed and swiped at her wet eyes. "Sure." By the time she'd exchanged places with Joshua, she didn't feel so weepy.

Mom told everyone, "We're going to call him Mattie while he's a baby, then Matt when he's growing up."

"Here's Mattie then, Ginger," Dr. Halstead said, putting him on the pillow on her lap.

He smelled clean and cosy, and she tried to hold him just right. As she watched, his lashes fluttered and his eyes opened. Blue eyes. Really bright blue. As they gazed at her, she felt jealousy disappearing and her heart filling with love. Her voice trembled as she said, "Hi, Mattie."

He blinked drowsily, then his blue eyes peered at her again. He was such a new little person, and she wanted him to be happy, for God's love to shine through her to him. Not caring if they all laughed at her, she said, again, "Hi, Mattie."

She darted a glance at her family. Lilabet smiled at her little brother as sweetly as a cherub; Joshua watched him tenderly, too; and Mom, Grant, and Grandfather glowed with happiness. Why had she worried so much when she'd already asked God to take away their jealousy? At this very moment God was changing things with His love.

Mattie stirred against her arm, and her eyes met his again. "Welcome to our family," she said.

He blinked as if he were taking that in.

"We're not perfect, Mattie," she explained, "but we're your family . . . and, even if we worried about your ruining everything, we see now that you could make things better yet."

She paused, and the wonder-working words came to her again. "You know what, Mattie Joshua Gabriel?"

He gurgled, almost as if he'd asked, "What?"

"We're all starting to love you, that's what," she told him. "Right here in this hospital . . . right this very minute, we're all starting to love you."

HERE COMES GINGER!

God, stop Mom's wedding!

Ginger's world is falling apart. Her mom has recently become a Christian and, even worse, has fallen in love with Grant Gabriel. Ginger can't stand the thought of leaving their little house near the beach . . . moving in with Grant and his two children . . . trading in her "brown cave of a bedroom" for a yellow canopied bed.

Ginger tries to fight the changes she knows are coming—green fingernails, salt in the sugar bowl, a near disaster at the beach. But she finds that change can happen inside her, too, when she meets the Lord her mom has come to trust.

The Ginger Series

Here Comes Ginger!	A Job for an Angel
Off to a New Start	Absolutely Green

ELAINE L. SCHULTE is a southern Californian, like Ginger. She has written many stories, articles, and books for all ages, but the **Ginger Trumbell Books** is her first series for kids.

Chariot Books™
David C. Cook Publishing Co.

OFF TO A NEW START

Aoooouuuuh! Aooooouuuuuh!

The blast of Ginger's conch shell sounds through the Gabriels' house. But is it a call to battle or a plea for peace?

Some days Ginger isn't sure, as she struggles to find her place in her new "combined" family, in her new school, and as a new child of God. With the wise counsel of Grandfather Gabriel and the support of her family, Ginger learns some important lessons about making friends and making peace.

The Ginger Series

- Here Comes Ginger!
- Off to a New Start
- A Job for an Angel
- Absolutely Green

ELAINE L. SCHULTE is a southern Californian, like Ginger. She has written many stories, articles, and books for all ages, but the **Ginger Trumbell Books** is her first series for kids.

A JOB FOR AN ANGEL

Love your neighbor?

October brings two new people into Ginger's life—and they couldn't be more different from each other.

Ginger looks forward to her Wednesday afternoon job of "baby-sitting" Aunt Alice. She may be elderly and ill, but she's cheerful and fun to be with. At school, however, Ginger is stuck trying to befriend grouchy Robin Lindberg, who never misses an opportunity to be nasty.

Ginger knows that "love your neighbor" includes the Robins as well as the Aunt Alices . . . but knowing doesn't make it easy. . . .

The Ginger Series

- Here Comes Ginger!
- Off to a New Start
- A Job for an Angel
- Absolutely Green

ELAINE L. SCHULTE is a southern Californian, like Ginger. She has written many stories, articles, and books for all ages, but the **Ginger Trumbell Books** is her first series for kids.

JUST VICTORIA

I am absolutely *dreading* junior high.

Vic and her best friend, Chelsie, have heard enough gory details about seventh grade to ruin their entire summer vacation. And as if school weren't a big enough worry, Vic suddenly finds problems at every turn:

• Chelsie starts hanging around Peggy Hiltshire, queen of all the right cliques, who thinks life revolves around the cheerleading squad.

• Vic's mom gets a "fulfilling" new job—with significantly less pay—at a nursing home.

• Grandma Warden is looking tired and pale—and won't see a doctor.

But Victoria Hope Mahoney has a habit of underestimating her own potential. The summer brings a lot of change, but Vic is equal to it as she learns more about her faith, friendship, and growing up.

Don't miss any books in The Victoria Mahoney Series!

#1 Just Victoria
#2 More Victoria
#3 Take a Bow, Victoria
#4 Only Kidding, Victoria
#5 Maybe It's Love, Victoria
#6 Autograph, Please, Victoria

SHELLY NIELSEN lives in Minneapolis, Minnesota, with her husband and two Yorkshire terriers.

MORE VICTORIA

Suddenly, life is nothing but problems.

Vic can see that there will be nothing dull about seventh grade . . . if she can only survive it.

First, there are the anonymous notes saying Corey Talbott, the rowdiest and most popular guy in the seventh grade has a crush on *her.* It's ridiculous, of course. But who could be writing them? And what will Vic do if Corey finds out?

Then, thanks again to the mysterious note sender, Victoria gets sent to the principal's office—the first time in her life she's faced such humiliation. What will her parents say? The last thing they need is one more thing to argue about . . . .

Live the ups and downs of Vic's first months of junior high in *More Victoria.*

Don't miss any books in The Victoria Mahoney Series!

#1 Just Victoria
#2 More Victoria
#3 Take a Bow, Victoria
#4 Only Kidding, Victoria
#5 Maybe It's Love, Victoria
#6 Autograph, Please, Victoria

SHELLY NIELSEN lives in Minneapolis, Minnesota, with her husband and two Yorkshire terriers.